MARGARET'S
MAMMOTH

HENRY GRANGER

ISBN 10-1986444813

Front cover painting by Larry Young

Cover graphics by Lesley Van Leeuwen-Vega

Interior illustrations by Laura Grafton

Back cover: Drawing of Great Lakes glaciers, U.S. Army Corps of Engineers

I wrote this story for my grandchildren.

To Adam, Brenda, Mason, Hayden, and Izzy. I hope you like the book as much as I did painting the front cover.

"Pap" (Larry)

In ancient times a herd of mammoths came to the salt licks and began the destruction of bear, deer, elk, buffalo, and other animals, which had been created for the use of the Indians. The Great Man above, looking down and seeing this, was so enraged that he seized his lightning, descended on the earth and hurled his bolts among the mammoths till the whole were slaughtered, except the big bull, who presenting his forehead to the shafts, shook them off as they fell; but the bull missed one bolt and it wounded him in the side; whereon, springing round, he bounded over the Ohio, over the Wabash, the Illinois, and finally over the great lakes, where he is living at this day.

— Thomas Jefferson, *Notes on the State of Virginia,*
Query VI (1787); reciting a Delaware Indian legend
about why mammoths disappeared from Virginia.

CHARACTERS

Margaret Gale	a modern girl, 10 years old
Butch	Margaret's cat
Joe Gale	Margaret's father
Nana	Margaret's grandmother
Mrs. Wydebottom	housekeeper
Miss Waxwurm	Margaret's teacher

Members of the Mammoth Clan

Oogay	husband of Tana, father of Tur and Mutt
Tana	wife of Oogay, mother of Tur and Mutt
Rom	Tana's brother, 16 years old
Tur	oldest son of Oogay and Tana, 12 years old
Mutt	younger son of Oogay and Tana, 7 years old
Gam	mother of Tana and Rom, grandmother of Tur and Mutt
baby girl	sister of Tur and Mutt
Stink	a small dog
Frik and Frak	big dogs

Members of the Lion Clan

Podi	Rom's girlfriend, 15 years old
Podi's father and mother	a married couple, older than Oogay and Tana

Member of the Beaver Clan

Bo	a suitor to Podi, 16 years old

Members of the Caribou Clan

three hunters	friends of Oogay
Chuz	a wrestler
boy with eagle feather	a helper
Tom	a Boy Scout camp counselor, 14 years old
two Boy Scouts	each 10 years old
nurse supervisor	woman in charge of the emergency room
Dr. Cardea	emergency room doctor

PART I
THE FAMILY

CHAPTER 1
TABBY CAT

A light rain was falling as Margaret sat beneath her bedroom window reading a book. Margaret's book told the story of the first artist to draw an animated cartoon animal. He had named his creation "Gertie the dinosaur." Margaret loved Gertie as she did all big animals.

The artist would stand on stage next to a giant moving picture of Gertie. The dinosaur was fat and friendly and did tricks. Margaret's cat, Butch, who was stretched out next to her on the floor, was also fat and friendly, but he would never perform tricks.

"Butch, can you say hello?" asked Margaret. At the sound of Margaret's voice Butch swiveled his head to look up at her and yawn. He was on his back so his furry orange face was upside down. Margaret was pretty sure that Butch thought tricks were beneath him. Only slobbery dogs did tricks.

Gertie's creator had grown up in Spring Lake, the same Michigan village where Margaret and her father lived. Their house was small and Margaret's room was a cozy space in the attic that had been painted and wallpapered by Margaret's mother before Margaret was born. Their back yard ended at a wave of cattails that lined the north bank of the Grand River. The river had flowed for more than ten thousand years, carrying silt down to Lake Michigan. The mouth of the river was two miles away. Downriver from Margaret's house was the landing where Margaret's father docked his trawler. Joe Gale worked for a university that was perched miles upstream on a higher riverbank. The university owned Joe's trawler and paid him to be the skipper.

Margaret and Joe lived alone. Margaret had no brothers or sisters. Margaret's mother had died before Margaret's first birthday, almost nine years ago. Margaret's parents had been canoeing as an angry thunderstorm formed out over Lake Michigan. The sky grew dark and straight-line winds came charging up the river faster than a speedboat. The canoe flipped over and only Joe made it to shore. Joe never talked about the day of the big storm, or about Margaret's mother. What Margaret knew about her mother she had learned from her Nana during Christmas and Easter visits to Detroit.

"Your mother had long, yellow curls like yours," Nana would say. "She was small-boned like you. And she was delightfully curious about the secrets of nature."

At Easter Margaret had asked, "Was my mother tall?"

"Oh yes, even taller than me!" Nana had replied with a grin. This was a joke because Nana was under five feet tall in her bare feet.

During summer vacation, a retired widow named Mrs. Wydebottom stayed at Margaret's house from eleven in the morning until four in the afternoon. She did light housekeeping, the laundry, and made lunch for Margaret. Mrs. Wydebottom lived alone except for a parakeet named Pretty Boy. Mrs. Wydebottom brought Pretty Boy to Margaret's house only once. Butch knocked over the bird's cage and Pretty Boy spent several hours flying from one high perch to another inside the house. When Joe got home he caught the bird with a fishing net and returned it to the cage. Mrs. Wydebottom left in a huff that day.

Mrs. Wydebottom was not mean to Margaret but she never took an interest in what Margaret was doing. Margaret was expected to keep herself amused while Mrs. Wydebottom tended to her chores. When Margaret sat down to eat lunch, Mrs. Wydebottom would leave her alone and go to the living room to watch the shopping network on television.

The summer rain had stopped by the time Joe got home from work. When the back storm slammed Margaret jumped up and ran downstairs to meet him. He was standing in the little porch that did double duty as a mud room and laundry room. She loved the way his work clothes smelled slightly of diesel fuel and silt. She squeezed Joe tightly around the waist and he bent down to kiss the part in her hair on the top of her head.

"And how was my precious treasure on this rainy Friday?" asked Joe in his rumbly voice. "Did Butch behave, or was he a bad cat?"

"Butch was mostly good today, Daddy. He wanted hot dogs for lunch but I told him to wait until you got home. So we had peanut butter and bananas instead. Can we make a campfire and cook the hot dogs for supper?"

"I don't see why not. While I get cleaned up, you put the dogs and buns and mustard in the little cooler and bring them out to the fire pit. I'll be there in a minute."

* * * * *

The blazing campfire made the hot dogs swell on their cooking sticks and split open. That's how Margaret knew they were done.

Margaret dropped a piece of her hot dog to the ground for Butch. The mottled tabby batted at the little chunk of meat with his paw until it cooled. Then he carried it into the tall weeds. Margaret could hear Butch making a "gnung, gnung" sound as he chewed.

"What did you do today, sweetheart?" asked Joe as he swallowed the last bite of his hot dog and dropped the roasting stick into the fire.

"Butch and I went down to the river bank to look for baby turtles. We didn't find none."

"Any," corrected Joe.

It was the time of year when the painted turtles climbed out of the water and onto the warm riverbank to dig their nests. Each mother turtle would lay seven to ten leathery eggs, cover them up with sand, and return to the water. When the tiny babies hatched they were on their own to make it back to the river. Most did not survive because they were eaten by birds or raccoons or foxes. Even Butch would catch and eat a baby turtle if Margaret was not quick enough to make him spit it out.

"Were there lots of turtles when you were little?" Margaret asked her father.

"More than now," Joe answered. "Aunt Sissy and I would ride our bikes up and down the muddy river road and collect hundreds of them. Your Grandma Gale always made us let them go at the end of the day."

"I wish I had a sister or a brother," said Margaret. Joe did not reply but stared into the fire.

The wind died down as the sun set and bats began to appear in the darkening sky. They were chasing mosquitoes and flying gnats. Last summer a bat had flown through the open window of Margaret's bedroom. Butch had grabbed the squeaking bat with his front paws and held it to the floor until Joe came upstairs and took it away from the cat. Joe showed the tiny prisoner to Margaret before throwing it back outside to fly away. The bat looked like a mouse with stretchy wings.

"People should not be afraid of this little guy," explained Joe. "He and his family eat a ton of bugs. If all the bats disappeared we might be carried away by the mosquitos!"

Margaret knew that Joe liked to exaggerate and she doubted mosquitos or any flying animal could lift a person off the ground. Still, tonight it was good that the bats were hunting the clouds of mosquitos that were buzzing just outside the smoke of the campfire.

Joe stood up to put another log on the fire. "I had a pretty interesting day," he told Margaret. "We went out on the big lake, not to take water samples but to watch for meteors."

"What is a mee-tee-or?" asked Margaret. The word was new to her so she pronounced it slowly.

"Well, in outer space there are a lot of rocks and big chunks of ice flying around. Sometimes a small piece will break away and come here because of Earth's gravity. Do you remember what gravity is?"

"Gravity makes things fall down."

"That's right, and a meteor is a piece of rock that falls toward Earth from outer space. Scientists at the university are excited because lately many meteors have been seen over Lake Michigan. The meteors make a bright light as they fall through the sky and my boss wanted us to take some pictures. So this week my boat was filled with lots of expensive cameras."

"Where did the meteors come from?"

"When you were little some scientists sent a rocket way up into the sky and it landed on a comet."

"A comet?"

"Oh, yes, well a comet is a large chunk of very old ice and rock. When the rocket landed on this comet, hundreds of pieces of the comet broke loose and headed toward Earth as meteors. Now, ten years later, some of those pieces are falling into Lake Michigan."

"How old is the comet?"

"Probably older than the Earth."

"Before animals?"

"Yes."

"And people?"

"Yes."

Margaret thought over what Joe had said. Then she asked, "Daddy, if you find a meteor, may I have it?"

He looked at his daughter and smiled. "Such a rare thing may have magical powers, so you'll need to be very careful." Joe wrapped one of his big hands around Margaret's waist while tickling under her arm with the other. She squealed and laughed and squirmed before stopping to give Joe a big hug.

"I love you, Daddy."

"I love you too. Time to put out the fire and go to bed."

* * * * *

Margaret could not sleep so she decided to work on a picture puzzle that was spread across the top of a card table at the end of her bed. She lay on her stomach, her head in her hands, and stared at the pieces. The cover of the puzzle box was her guide. The cover was decorated with wonderfully strange animals standing at the edge of a thick forest. Each kind of animal was identified by a gold label with black letters. Flat headed, hairy elephants called *mastodons* were reaching into the tree branches with their trunks and stuffing leaves into their mouths. Bigger elephants with round heads and even longer hair, called *mammoths*, trudged single file through tall grass as they grazed on the stalks beneath their broad bellies. The mastodons and the mammoths were being stalked by two saber tooth cats called *smilodons*.

At school Margaret had learned that the animals in the puzzle were extinct, which meant they had lived a long time ago and all had died before Nana or George Washington or even Jesus was born. Margaret's teacher, Miss Waxwurm, told the class that wild people hunted the big creatures until they were all gone.

Margaret liked the mammoths best so she worked on that part of the puzzle first. A mammoth family appeared as she snapped more pieces into place. Three shaggy, grown-up mammoths were following one another, the biggest in front and a baby between the other two adults. The grown-ups were dark brown but the baby was yellow, its hair almost the same color as Margaret's hair. The grown-ups' tusks were long and curved like part of a circle.

Margaret turned her attention to the mastodons. There were five, some bigger than others, but no baby. Their coats were shorter than the mammoths', and medium grey in color. They also had long tusks, twisted more than curved.

There were no people in the puzzle so Margaret could not tell if the mammoths and mastodons were bigger or smaller than the elephant she had seen at the circus. Margaret's Girl Scout troop had earned the price of admission by selling cookies, and the best part of the show had been an Asian elephant named Old Doc. He did tricks, including lifting a tree trunk covered with monkeys. Old Doc's shoulder was as tall as the top of Joe's head. The elephant had hair but it was not thick like the coat of a mastodon or mammoth.

Butch, who had been sleeping next to Margaret's pillow, woke up and padded over to see what she was doing. Butch reached out a paw to poke at the puzzle pieces that made up the smilodons. His orange fur matched the coats of the saber tooth cats.

"No! Bad cat!" said Margaret as she scooped up Butch and rose to open her bedroom door. As she dropped the big tabby onto the landing at the top of the stairs, Joe called up from the living room.

"Margaret, are you OK? Do you need something?"

"No, Daddy, I'm fine. Butch is being a pest so I'm sending him down to bother you."

"Alright, good night then."

"Good night, Daddy."

Her eyelids were getting heavy so she decided to lie down and listen to the night sounds through her open window. She fell asleep as soon as her head hit the pillow.

CHAPTER 2
METEOR

Margaret woke up to the smell of pancakes. It was Sunday and Joe's day off from work. Joe had not taken Margaret to church since the funeral of Margaret's mother. Instead, Joe always made them a big pancake breakfast on Sunday. Afterwards, weather permitting, they went fishing.

"Morning, sleepyhead," called Joe as Margaret shuffled into the kitchen wearing a pink tee shirt and yellow pajama pants covered with drawings of tigers. Nana had bought the pants for Margaret after they had watched a pair of Amur tigers playing in a shallow pond at the Detroit Zoo.

Butch was sitting patiently below the stove, hoping for a tasty morsel. Sometimes Joe would drop a bit of bacon to the floor on purpose.

"Morning, Daddy," yawned Margaret. She sat down at her plate to discover a golden pancake staring up at her. The pancake was shaped like Mickey Mouse's head, a round face and two round ears. The eyes were raisins and the mouth was a line of chocolate chips. The Mickey Mouse pancake had been Margaret's favorite breakfast when she was little, but lately anything to do with Mickey Mouse made her feel like a baby. She didn't mention it because she did not want to hurt Joe's feelings.

Margaret poured a drop of maple syrup on each of Mickey's eyes and a line of the sweet stuff along his mouth. As she took her first bite Joe sat down next to her with his own stack of pancakes in one hand and a plate of bacon in the other. He passed a crisp strip of bacon to Margaret.

"I think this morning we'll fish below Probst's Island," said Joe. "One of the boys at the bait shop claims big walleye are hanging around a brush pile at the downstream end of the island. We'll take the john boat and anchor by that brush pile."

"Sounds good," Margaret replied as she swallowed her first bite of bacon. "I'll bring along some gum drops so we can try for catfish if the walleye aren't bitin'."

Margaret was pretty good at catching big barbed catfish with her gum drops. 'Gum drops' were bait made from her own secret recipe. She stirred corn flakes, molasses, powdered cheese, and a spoon full of garlic powder into a gooey paste. She rolled the paste into little balls and placed them in the freezer to harden. Margaret usually brought a dozen gum drops with her in the john boat. Once they were anchored over a promising spot in the river, Joe would tie a large hook to the end of the line on Margaret's fishing pole. He would pass the hook through a gum drop and place a lead sinker on the line ahead of the hook, to make sure that the ball of bait sank to the bottom. Catfish have a powerful sense of smell that helped them find the stinky gum drop. Once the bait was on the bottom, all you had to do was sit still and wait.

The thought of fishing made Margaret lose interest in her breakfast. She did not finish her pancake and dropped the last of her bacon to Butch, who had been rubbing himself between the legs of her chair to attract attention.

"What's the matter, did I burn Mickey?" Joe asked.

"No, my pancake was fine. I'm just not very hungry this morning."

"Well, that's a shame because, you know . . ."

Margaret finished Joe's sentence for him " . . . pancakes are the first bread ever made by people." Joe had told her many times how Indians used hot flat stones like a frying pan to cook bread pancakes. Joe knew a lot about Indians. Last summer he had driven a team of scientists to Lake Huron and Saginaw Bay. The scientists were looking for clues about how the earliest Indians, called "ancient people," hunted for food. Joe explained to Margaret that the ancient people lived before stories were written in letters or drawn in paint. They were mighty hunters even though their only tools were made of wood, bone, and a sharp stone called "chert." Joe brought home a small chert spear point from that trip and gave it to Margaret. She wore it on a beaded thread around her neck every day.

"Can I wear what I've got on to go fishin'?" asked Margaret as she picked up her plate and brought it to the sink. "I don't want to get gum drop smell on my good clothes, and my PJs are easy to wash."

"Fine with me," answered Joe as he washed and rinsed her plate. "Be sure to wear your old sneakers and your life jacket. Bag up the gum drops while I make some coffee. Grab some apples and a bottle of water too. Put Butch outside and meet me at the boat."

Half an hour later they were sitting in the flat-bottomed john boat, Joe at the oars and Margaret perched in the bow. The stern of the little pram was tied to a brush pile, which left the square bow free to swing in the current. If walleye were lurking at the bottom, they did not seem interested in the shiners that Joe and Margaret were using for bait. The morning sun was getting hot so Joe let Margaret take off her life jacket and use it as a seat cushion. She had also kicked off her sneakers. It was only the middle of June but already Margaret was tan like the girl on the Coppertone bottle.

Her hair bleaches out in the summertime, thought Joe, *just like her mom.*

"Whattaya say we put down a hand line for catfish, baited with one or two of your gum drops?" Joe asked.

"Good idea. I'm tired of just watching the bobber on my pole."

Joe quickly rigged the hand line, tied two big hooks at the end, squeezed on a blob made from three gum drops, and tossed the entire mess out toward the middle of the river. The weighted hooks soon sank to the bottom.

"You want me to tie the line off to an oarlock?"

"No, Daddy, I'd rather hold on to the line so I can feel any tugs."

"Okay, but don't wrap the end tightly around your wrist. You might get a rope burn if a big lunker takes the bait."

"I know, I know," Margaret replied testily. They had set hand lines many times before, Joe always warned about rope burns, and they never hooked anything big enough to worry about. Margaret tied a loop at the end of the hand line and slipped it over her fingers to her wrist. *That should be loose enough*, she thought.

By noon the sun was blazing and they had not caught a single fish. Joe pulled the john boat up on the sandy shore of Probst's Island so they could get out and stretch their legs. He spread old cattail stalks on the soggy sand so they would have a dry place to sit, then stuck more smelly gum drops on Margaret's hand line and tossed it out into deep water. Joe lay down, his hands behind his head and his ball cap pulled low over his eyes. Margaret sat cross-legged next to him, the end of her line once again looped around her wrist.

A blue heron appeared from behind some bushes, slowly creeping along in the shallow water on long thin legs. The heron was the biggest of all the birds on the river and a tremendous fisherman. He could stand for hours without making a sound, and when a careless fish swam too close he would spear it with his long beak. If something scared the heron, he would fly away on his powerful long wings while screaming a terrible squawk.

As the heron came to a halt on one leg, flashes of light began to appear in the clear blue sky, as if somebody were shooting off fireworks in the middle of the day. Joe stood and pointed up, saying, "Look, Margaret, a new meteor shower is starting."

"There are so many!" Margaret exclaimed. "You think any will reach the ground?"

She could not hear her father's reply because at that exact moment the heron sprang into the air and flew away with a thundering "Kee-kaw-yaw-yaw!" Behind the big bird the water erupted. A glimmering meteor, millions of years old and no larger than a baseball, had crashed into the river near the end of Margaret's hand line. A deep hole opened in the river bottom and a gush of muddy water climbed into the air. Startled, Joe tripped backwards and fell hard to the ground.

As Margaret leaped up to help Joe, the loop around her wrist tightened and she was yanked away from her father and into the river. She fought to stay out of the deep water by digging her heels in the mud, but whatever was on the other end of the line was too powerful for her to resist. She barely had time to yell, "Help!" before she was dragged under the surface and disappeared.

CHAPTER 3
PEOPLE

Margaret opened her eyes in the cloudy water because something was slapping her in the face. It was the tail of a fish with black fins and deep blue scales. The fish was so long that she could barely see the barbs flowing back from each side of its monstrous big head.

I've hooked a giant catfish! Margaret was so startled she almost quit holding her breath.

The big fish dived toward a dark hole that had opened when the meteor hit the river bottom. Mysterious red bubbles came zipping out of the hole like sparks from a campfire. The water smelled minty, then like burnt toast. Margaret could feel the water growing colder as she was pulled through the red bubbles and deeper into the underwater crater.

I must get loose or I'll drown! she thought.

With her free hand Margaret tugged her necklace over her head. She found the chert spear point with her fingers and used it to saw at the fishing line around her other wrist. The line broke and the catfish disappeared. Her lungs burning, Margaret kicked out of the cave and toward the surface.

She broke the surface coughing and gasping for air. Margaret could feel the warm sun on the top of her head. Her long blond hair was plastered across her face so it was hard to see. *That catfish must have pulled me a long way,* Margaret thought, *because I hear children laughing*. Margaret swam toward the voices and stood up when she reached shallow water.

She could not believe her eyes. She had made it back to the island but the john boat was gone and Joe was nowhere to be seen. Tall willow trees were growing on the island where only cattails had grown before. And standing along the beach were *people* unlike any Margaret had ever seen.

Two men stood next to a campfire. They were covering the fire with wet leaves to make a lot of smoke. Strips of catfish were hanging from sharp poles that leaned over the fire. A lean-to had been built a few paces away from the fire.

One of the men looked to be about Joe's age, but it was hard to tell for sure because his face was covered with checkerboard tattoos. The other man was younger, maybe a teenager, and his face had no decorations unless you counted pimples. Both had brown eyes, straight black hair worn down to their shoulders, and skin the color of caramel candy. The men were a head shorter than Joe but they had broad chests and were well muscled. It was plain to see they had tattoos on their arms and legs, because the men were naked except for loin cloths made from animal hide.

Two laughing boys came running up to the fire. One looked like he might be Margaret's age, the other two or three years younger. They had been chasing each other through the willow trees and their long black hair was covered with seed fluff. Like the men they wore no clothes except for rough underwear. Margaret noticed that the older boy had a star shaped birthmark behind his right eye. He wore a string of small shells around his neck, which made Margaret realize she was still clutching her spear point necklace. Unclenching her fist, she pulled the keepsake back over her head.

The men and boys stared at Margaret, and she stared back, wet and shivering.

"Is it a water spirit, Da?" the smaller boy asked the older man.

"Its skin is so white; I bet it's a ghost!" added the older boy.

The men said nothing but slowly reached to the ground and picked up heavy pieces of firewood, while never taking their eyes off Margaret.

"Put down those clubs!" It was a woman's voice. An old woman, shorter than Nana, hobbled out from the lean-to, around the fire, and into the river until she was face to face with Margaret.

"Be careful, Gam," the younger man called out, "it might bite you and drag you into the water."

The old woman glared back at the men and boys. "Can't you see it's only a child? She's freezing from being in the river. Stand back so she'll come up to the fire." The old woman held out a hand and said softly, "Come here girl, I won't hurt you."

Margaret knew she should be terrified, but the old woman seemed so – nice. She was the same color as the men, and barefoot. "Gam" wore a jumper of deer skin that covered from below her neck to just above her knees. Her hair was silver grey and hung in two braids to her shoulders. Bits of bone and tiny twigs had been carefully woven into the braids. Her face and neck were covered with deep wrinkles. Gam wore several necklaces made of shells and had lines of tiny stars tattooed at her wrists and ankles. When Gam held out her hand, Margaret could see that she also had a tattoo on the heel of her thumb. It was a little mammoth.

Gam gently wrapped an arm around Margaret's shoulders and led her past the staring menfolk, around the fire and into the lean-to. A young woman about the age of Miss Waxwurm was lying on her side on soft grass, the top of her jumper pulled down just far enough so she could feed the baby girl lying next to her. The baby was making happy "mm, mm, mm," noises while it nursed.

"Well, Gam, what creature is this?" asked the young mother.

"I'm not a 'creature'," Margaret blurted out. "I'm a girl!"

"And a very wet one!" proclaimed Gam. In the blink of an eye she pulled off Margaret's dripping pajamas and headed out the door of the lean-to. "Tana, I'll hang her clothes over the fire to dry and bring you back a nice piece of smoked fish."

"Thank you, Gam," replied the young mother.

The infant had finished nursing and Tana bounced her baby gently until she burped. Tana carefully slid the little one into a soft bag of woven grass and the baby immediately fell asleep, snoring. Tana looked at Margaret and said, "Come here, water mouse."

Margaret hesitantly stepped forward and dropped to the ground next to Tana. Cold water dripped down Margaret's back, which made her start shivering again. Tana hugged Margaret to warm her, rocking back and forth on the ground, singing, "Coo-coo, little mouse, mother's here, coo-coo-coo." Margaret, feeling lost and exhausted, began to softly sob while Tana stroked Margaret's hair to wring out the water. A moment later Margaret stopped crying and was fast asleep like the baby.

* * * * *

The sun was low in the sky when Margaret awoke and peeked out of the lean-to. Somebody had dressed her while she slept. Her pajamas were dry and smelled strongly of wood smoke. The smell made her think of backyard campfires with Joe, and for a moment she was afraid she would begin crying again.

"Come here, girl, and eat." It was Gam, motioning to Margaret while removing a piece of smoked fish from above what was left of the cooking fire. Sitting cross-legged around the fire were Tana with the baby in her lap, the older and younger men, and the two boys. Piled next to the boys were three of the homeliest dogs Margaret had ever seen. The dogs had rough brindle coats, stocky bodies, pointy ears and curly tails. The smallest dog looked like one of his ears had been bitten off. The dogs eyed Margaret but made no sound.

"Tur, give this to our new friend," ordered Gam as she handed a big piece of white fish to the older boy. Tur did as he was told and marched right up to Margaret, slapping the fish in her hands while muttering, "Here, this is for you. It's the *best* piece so hope you like it." He turned and sat down again next to the men.

"Thank you," Margaret replied shyly. She took a bite of the greasy fish. It tasted wonderful! She took a bigger bite and the adults began to grin.

"Slow down, girl, I'm not sure I found all the bones," warned Gam.

The smaller boy jumped up and ran over to Margaret. He reached out and touched the leg of her pajama bottoms while asking, "Do you have a name? Mine's Mutt."

"Of course I have a name, it's Margaret!" She swatted Mutt's little hand away from her pant leg.

"That's my brother, Tur," Mutt said, pointing to the older boy. "We have a baby sister." Next he pointed to the men. "My da is Oogay, he's a great hunter. Rom is my uncle and he taught me to throw a fishing stick. My ma is Tana and my gam is Gam and . . ."

Margaret shut Mutt up with a question: "What is the baby's name?"

"Everyone knows a baby don't have a name," Tur announced from his seat near the fire. "Ma and Da will name her after she starts to walk."

The littlest dog got up, stretched, and trotted over to see if Margaret might give him a scrap of her catfish dinner. Margaret held her meal a little higher than before, and asked "What's this dog's name?"

"Stink," replied Rom. It was the first thing the young man had said to anyone else in the family since Margaret's arrival. "If you feed him some of that greasy fish you'll find out why. The others are Frik and Frak," he said, pointing to each in turn. Apparently the biggest dog was Frik.

"Where are your parents and your clan, Margaret?" asked Oogay. He was reclining on one elbow and picking his teeth with a pine needle held between the fingers of his free hand. "How'd you get here? Do you have a raft?"

"No, not a raft, but a boat. I was fishing with Joe – my da – when I was pulled into deep water by a big, big fish. When I got lose and kicked to the surface, Joe was gone and you were here. That's all I know."

"Well, we can't leave the child to be eaten by lions or wolves," Gam declared. "She can come with us and maybe find her clan at the Gathering. Maybe 'Joe' would like to make a marriage for his daughter."

"Oh, gross!" howled Mutt. He and his brother fell into a laughing fit.

I agree, thought Margaret.

"We will leave as soon as the sun rises," Oogay announced. "Everyone pack your things before sunset so there is no delay in the morning." Without discussion the family rose and began to make piles of possessions and tools.

The family owned more things than Margaret had realized. Each of the men would carry several long spears; also leather shoulder bags filled with fishing nets, spare chert to make points and scrapers, and decorative necklaces to be worn at important occasions like the Gathering. Each boy was expected to carry a handful of short spears and a wooden sling with which to throw them, plus a hip pouch to hold their personal totems. Tana had a shoulder bag made from a deer's stomach in which she carried bone needles, twine, two small chert knives, and willow fluff to use like a diaper inside the baby's carry basket. Gam had two shoulder bags, one filled with plant medicines and colored earth to make body paint, the other filled with a piece of carved mammoth ivory and some tiny bird's bones that she used to predict the future. Three piles were assembled for the dogs, who would carry the family's cold weather clothes, extra food, and dry fire starting tinder. When darkness came the work ended and Oogay's people settled down for the night.

Everyone slept in their clothes, on the ground. Tana held the baby in her arms while she nestled next to Oogay in the lean-to. Tur and Mutt slept in a snoring pile with the dogs. Rom slept by himself with his spear at his side. Gam had Margaret sleep close to her. The old lady woke every two or three hours to feed the fire and study the stars, but Margaret never stirred.

CHAPTER 4
CLAN

The next morning the family rose at dawn as Oogay had commanded. The river was less than three feet deep between the island and the closest riverbank so it was easy to walk across to the mainland. The water was too deep for the dogs to wade, but Frik, Frak and Stink were good swimmers.

The family walked from sunrise to sunset, toward the rising sun and always with the riverbank in sight on their right. Oogay permitted one stop in the morning, another when the sun was highest in the sky, and a third in mid-afternoon. During the stops the dogs were untied from their bundles and allowed to wander, but they obediently returned when Rom whistled. Tana nursed the baby while Gam gave each person a ball of smoked meat and pine nuts to munch on. Much attention was given to feet. Chiggers and ticks were removed and tears in moccasins repaired. Going to the bathroom was a private affair, behind any convenient tree. Margaret longed for the simple pleasure of toilet paper.

During the noon break Margaret sat down next to Tur and Mutt. "What is the Gathering?" she asked Tur.

Tur pretended not to hear the question.

"I found this while we were walking. If you tell me about the Gathering you may have it." Margaret held out her arm and opened her hand. In her palm was the skin of a dragonfly nymph, tinted blue and green as if painted by fairies. The boys drew close to look at the little treasure.

"Wow," exclaimed Mutt, "That's a really nice one, bigger than any we've found. Tell her, Tur, tell Margaret about the Gathering."

"All right," sighed Tur, "but you can keep your dead bug."

"I'll take it!" squeaked Mutt. Margaret pointed her upturned hand toward the little boy, and he snatched the nymph skin and went skipping off to show it to his ma.

Margaret turned to Tur, leaned close to him and said, "So?" Tur did not like a girl being so familiar. He stood and crossed his arms before speaking.

"Our family belongs to the Clan of the Mammoth. There are many families in our clan. The clan gathers every twelve moons, when the weather is warm. There are games and feasts. We learn who has died since the last Gathering. Gifts are exchanged and sometimes marriages are made. Most of all, the men work together to make tools from the stone that is scattered on the ground."

"What sort of tools?"

"Spear points of all sizes, like the one you wear around your neck. And knives and saws and scrapers. Don't you know anything?"

"Don't get snippy with me, mister!" At that Margaret stood and ran over to see what Gam was doing. Tur watched her go, arms still crossed and mouth open.

Gam was rubbing a pale white deer hide with salt. As Margaret approached, the old lady rolled up the hide and stuffed it in one of the dog bundles.

"What are you making, Gam?"

"Something for you, maybe," chuckled Gam. "Come closer and stand still."

Margaret stood straight with her arms at her sides. Gam pulled some long leather strings from a bag on the ground. She looped one of the strings around Margaret at the shoulders, then tied a knot at one end to mark the distance. Gam repeated the process with another string around Margaret's waist. Finally, Gam used a shorter string to measure the distance from Margaret's belly button to her knees.

"There, that should do," Gam decided. "Time to get moving. Why don't you ask Tana if you can carry something for her? The baby gets heavy as the day grows older." Margaret did as she was told, and Tana was happy for the help.

At night the family gathered around a fire to eat the largest meal of the day, which was roasted cattail roots and some crayfish that Tur had found under a rock along the river bank. There was also a fried mudpuppy. Rom had spied the big salamander in shallow water and speared it with a stick. It fried up nicely when laid upon hot stones at the bottom of the fire.

After supper stories were told and there was much laughing and teasing. Margaret wished she could understand all of the jokes, but still it was comforting to be with a group of people who loved each other.

As the fire died down Mutt nuzzled up to Tana. The little boy's eyelids started to grow heavy as he begged, "Da, tell us again about the big bull mammoth." It was Mutt's favorite story.

Oogay rolled his eyes at Tana, but she said, "Yes, Da, let's hear that story, it's such a good one."

With a small sigh Oogay stood up and began the story. "Long, long ago, before people, all the animals of the earth were ruled by the mammoths."

"Even the long toothed lions?" yawned Mutt.

"Yes, even the lions did not dare bother the mammoths, because in those days the mammoths ate meat as well as grass, and a nice juicy lion was one of their favorite snacks."

"Rom told me that lion meat does not taste very good," interrupted Mutt.

"Well, maybe not, but still no lion would attack a mammoth for fear of being gobbled up." Mutt accepted the explanation and Oogay continued.

"The biggest bull was a giant, twice as big as any mammoth who had ever lived. He was very old and very wise and knew where to find the greenest grass and the sweetest water. In those days most of the Big Ice - -"

"What's the Big Ice?" Margaret whispered to Gam.

"Shush," Gam whispered back, "listen to the story and I'll tell you about the Big Ice later."

"- - was thicker than the white pine is tall, but around its edges it was thin and dangerous. Big animals would sometimes walk on the thin ice and fall through, never to be seen again.

"One day a baby mammoth, not more than a year old, wandered away from its mother and onto thin ice. The ice began to crack and the baby became stranded. The baby called out in the mammoth tongue, 'I'm afraid to move and my toes are freezing. Mother, save me!'

"The frantic mother rushed out onto the thin ice, fell through and disappeared. The big bull knew it was too dangerous for him or any of the other adults to brave the ice. The scared baby stood alone, frantically trumpeting to the adults.

"The big bull turned toward the north wind and called out, 'O great spirit of the north, save our precious baby!'

"The north wind felt sorry for the bull and cast a spell over him. The bull fell to the ground in a deep sleep and while he slept one of his huge tusks turned into a boy and the other into a girl. They were the very first members of our clan. The boy and girl slowly walked onto the ice, which did not crack beneath their small weight. When they reached the baby mammoth they climbed upon its back and guided it over solid ice back to the herd. From that day and ever after, the people of our clan have been friends to the mammoths. We do not hunt mammoths, and we have their permission to collect the old tusks of their ancestors."

"Where do you find the tusks?" asked Margaret.

"There is a special place where the old, old mammoths go to die," Gam answered. "Tusks lie amid piles of bones in the mammoth graveyard."

"Gam can read the stars so she knows how to find the mammoth graveyard," mumbled Mutt. A second later he was asleep with his head in his mother's lap.

"Is that true, Gam?" said Margaret.

"I suppose it is, child. After we reach the Gathering, you and I will visit the mammoth graveyard to collect tusks. They are good for trading with the other clans."

"Other clans?"

"There are four clans," Rom explained. He held up four fingers to make his point. It was the first time he had spoken since supper. "The Clans of the Mammoth, Beaver, Lion, and Caribou will all be at the Gathering. All clans make things from mammoth tusk, but only our clan is permitted to collect them."

The fire was dying down so the family began to bed down for the night. The moon was full and cast a soft glow upon everything. There was enough light for Margaret to watch Gam walk down to the river. Gam removed something from a bag around her shoulder and held it up with both arms toward the Moon.

"Mother Moon," Gam chanted, "thank you for guiding our family to another Gathering. Please watch over us and keep us safe."

During Gam's chanting Margaret quietly walked up next to the old woman. Gam handed something heavy to Margaret. In the dim light Margaret could see it was a piece of mammoth tusk, about a foot long, carefully inscribed with many little cuts and a row of twelve tiny holes. A delicate peg of bone, no wider than a toothpick, was stuck in one of the holes. "Stand still," Gam told Margaret. Gam carefully plucked the peg out of the tusk and placed it in the next hole. "The Gathering will take place before Mother Moon hides her face again," explained Gam.

Later that night Margaret dreamed that she watched while a meteor fell from the sky and made a dark hole in the Big Ice. She could hear Joe's voice calling to her from inside the hole. "Please come home, Margaret, please!"

CHAPTER 5
BEAVER

The family continued to follow the river. Now and then the river jogged to the north or south, but it mostly it stretched to the east. Every morning Oogay's camp was ten miles farther upriver than the day before.

As she walked Margaret noticed that the trees growing along the river were the same as grew in the old Spring Lake cemetery, but they were much, much bigger. The white pines and hemlocks stretched so far up into the sky that is was difficult to see the treetops from the ground. Their bottoms were so wide that four people standing in a circle, arms outstretched, could not lock hands around the trunks. The forest floor was dark and moist because the tall trees only permitted an occasional sunbeam to reach the ground. Fallen giants made of rotting wood were everywhere, covered in moss and vines.

Most of the forest birds were familiar to Margaret, but there were more of them flying about and calling to each other than back home. Gam seemed to know every bird by its song.

At the end of the third day the family stopped next to a rapids made of big round stones. After the children collected enough firewood to last the night, Tana gave them permission to go down to the rapids, "But be back before the sun sets."

The rapids were wide but not tall. Still, the rushing water frothed and roared as it pushed its way around the rocks. As Tur, Margaret, and Mutt stood shoulder to shoulder taking it all in, Mutt pointed and exclaimed, "Some of the big rocks are moving!"

"Those aren't rocks, dummy, those are beavers," corrected Tur. "Let's get closer."

They quietly made their way down to the water's edge and hid behind a tree trunk that was half sunk in the mud. Thirty feet away, more or less in the middle of the river, were two giant beavers. *They're each as big as a washing machine,* thought Margaret.

Both beavers were covered from snout to backside with coarse, oily red fur. They had webbed feet and thick nails. Their tails were long and hairless, but not wide and flat.

The beavers stood on their hind legs in the water below the rapids and patiently waited for clumps of weeds and sod to cascade around the boulders and into their waiting arms. The beavers held the floating vegetation to their chests with their front paws while poking through the soggy mess with their muzzles. It was a salad bar for beavers.

The big rodents had excellent eyesight and knew they were being watched by the children. They didn't seem to mind. But after a few minutes both beavers turned and stared across the water to the other side of the river. There, partly hidden in the dark underbrush, were three almost-grown dire wolves.

During winter nights, when sound traveled a long way on the wind, Tur had heard dire wolves howling at the moon. This was his first look at one in person. They were bigger than timber wolves and had slightly longer fur. Their coats were dark grey but in the shadows they looked black as night. "I bet those three are brothers from the same litter," Tur whispered to Mutt and Margaret. The parent wolves were nowhere to be seen.

The wolves carefully edged their way to the bank of the river, their eyes fixed on the beavers. The beavers stared back. One of the wolves started to whine, exciting the others to pace back and forth. After a few minutes one of the wolves gathered himself and jumped for the nearest boulder that poked out of the water. He made it, but not for long.

All of the boulders in the river were slick as ice because they were covered with algae. When the young wolf landed on the boulder his paws slid out from under him and he flew head first into the cold water. He kicked and struggled to make it back to shore, where he stood panting and dripping wet. He gave himself a great shake and most of the water flew away. The other two wolves proceeded to sniff their brother all over, as if to make sure he was not injured.

Meanwhile, the beavers began to swim downstream, occasionally looking back at the wolves. The wolves did not follow but stayed where they were, yipping and barking at the retreating beavers.

Tur, Mutt, and Margaret jogged along the riverbank in an effort to keep pace with the swimming beavers. Tur was fastest and led the way. He wanted to see where the beavers lived. Rom had taught Tur that giant beavers do not build dams or live in huts made of sticks. Instead, like a muskrat, they dig dens in the banks of ponds and rivers. The door to a den is almost always under water.

The beavers made their way toward a big white cedar that had blown over with its roots exposed to the river. They stopped in front of the toppled tree, in about two feet of water. The beaver closest to the shore took a deep breath and disappeared under the water. "He's going inside his den," yelled Tur.

As the second beaver began to take a deep breath, a blur of black fur and white teeth rocketed from behind the fallen cedar and landed on top of the startled beaver. The attacker was Alpha, father of the three young wolves. The big male wrapped his strong jaws around the beaver's throat and pulled back so that the beaver could not dive. As the two big animals struggled, an adult she-wolf rushed into the water and bit down on one of the beaver's hind legs.

The teeth of the wolves were like daggers, and soon the water around the beaver was red with blood. The beaver tried to shake off his attackers but his strength was failing because of his wounds.

Slowly, without ever letting go, the parent wolves used their combined weight to push the beaver under the water. After a few minutes the beaver quit struggling. He had drowned.

Alpha and his mate pulled the giant beaver up to the edge of the river bank and lay panting across the carcass. Alpha threw back his head and howled. Margaret could see that the left side of Alpha's face was covered with a pure white blaze. The three brothers came running to join their parents for a meal.

Margaret and the boys had stood behind a pussy willow shrub while they silently watched the wolves make the kill. In all the excitement they hadn't noticed that the sun was setting. Suddenly, a deep voice made them jump and turn around.

"Wolves are smart." The speaker was Oogay. He was standing on a tree stump above the children. Rom stood silently next to Oogay. Both men were carrying spears. The dogs were with them. Little Stink, always ready for a fight, stared across the river at the wolves and growled.

"The parent wolves planned the attack," Oogay continued. "The pups were sent to bother the beavers so they would swim home. Their father knew that the beavers had dug the door to their den in shallow water. That was the beavers' mistake, and now the wolves will have beaver to eat for a week."

"A clever hunter is the most dangerous hunter," Rom added.

"Time to return to camp," said Oogay. "When your mother is worried about you she is more ferocious than a she-wolf."

* * * * *

It rained off and on for two days and nights after the dire wolves attacked the giant beaver. The river rose and became much wider. Oogay decided to move deeper into the forest so that the family could continue to walk on solid ground.

During the day the men went hunting and everyone else tried to stay dry under the thick leafy branches of a sweet viburnum bush. At night the family huddled together at the base of a large pine. They cut saplings and jammed them in the lower limbs for a leafy roof. A small fire kept away the worst of the night shivers. Margaret felt cold and miserable in her tattered pajamas but she kept quiet because the others took the bad weather in stride.

Occasionally the rain would stop for a few minutes. Gam and Tana would use the dry moments to unroll Gam's deer hide, scrape off the salt, soak it in rain water, wring it out, then smoke it over the fire. The steps of soaking, wringing and smoking were repeated several times. Margaret helped with the wringing out of the wet hide. She could tell that the skin became more supple and slightly darker in color every time it was smoked.

In the afternoon of the second rainy day, Margaret was passing time trying to teach Stink to sit up and roll over. He liked the attention but the lessons did not sink in.

"Margaret," it was Gam calling, "leave that smelly dog alone and come here please." Margaret did as she was told.

Gam was standing beside the drying fire and holding something behind her back. Tana was sitting on the ground nursing the baby. The two women glanced at each other and smiled at Margaret.

"Come closer, girl, and strip off those rags that used to be clothes."

What was left of Margaret's pajamas fell to the ground. Gam kicked them to the side. "We'll wash these and keep them for when the days become shorter and colder."

Gam produced a garment from behind her back and held it up to Margaret. It was a deer skin shift, similar to those worn by Tana and Gam. The little dress had been sown together from two pieces of Gam's deer hide. Just under the neckline, tacked to the fabric with tiny stitches, was a circle of eight shiny pebbles.

"Try it on," said Gam.

Margaret pulled the dress over her head. It fit exactly.

"Thank you, Gam, thank you!" exclaimed Margaret as she threw her arms around the old woman and hugged. *I am so happy not to be wearing grubby pajamas!* thought Margaret.

"I made these for you." Tana held up a pair of deerskin moccasins that matched the dress. "Wear them when the ground is rocky or the snow comes." Margaret tried on the moccasins and they also fit nicely. "I measured your feet when you were sleeping," confessed Tana.

"Thank you, Tana," Margaret whispered. She did not want to wake the baby, who had finished eating and was sound asleep. Tana slid the babe back into her carrying basket and stood up. "Stand still," she told Margaret.

Tana had a wooden comb in her hand. She carefully ran it through Margaret's long yellow curls. In a few places there were tangles that Gam had to cut out with a sharp piece of chert. Next the two women began to make a braid on each side of Margaret's head. Gam produced a small pouch of dried chokecherry blossoms and proceeded to weave them into the braids. Gam stood back to examine their handiwork.

"Now you look like a beautiful maiden, and will make the right impression on the older boys at the Gathering." Gam's pronouncement startled Margaret. She hiccupped nervously.

"Don't worry," said Tana, "you still have several years left to run and roam with Tur and Mutt. Why don't you go show the boys your new clothes?"

Margaret gratefully skipped away. The rain was starting again. She found the boys huddled under a temporary hut they had made from pieces of a rotting pine stump.

"Margaret, wha' happened to you?" exclaimed Mutt.

"Ma and Gam turned her into a girl," marveled Tur.

"I fink you look pretty," said Mutt. In the last several days Mutt had lost both of his top front baby teeth and it affected his pronunciation.

"What do you think?" Margaret asked Tur, twirling so he could see her new braids.

"I think . . . I think I'd better find some dry firewood before Da and Rom come back from their hunt." Tur stood and wandered away, pretending to look for kindling.

Margaret felt hurt, but she didn't know why.

* * * * *

When the rain finally stopped the family packed up and headed again to the east. The forest floor was a blanket of flowers, including a thousand pink orchids. As the family walked through the blooms Margaret told Gam, "My dad calls these moccasin flowers." Thinking about Joe gave Margaret a lump in her throat.

"We call them dancing hearts," Gam replied. "Do you see those tiny white flowers on the bramble bushes ahead of us?"

"Yes."

"Well, those are the blooms of the black raspberry. There would have been earlier blooms, so if you hunt between the new flowers you should find berries ripe for eating. When we stop for the midday meal you and the boys can go berry picking. Be sure to wear your new moccasins in the prickles."

Lunch was a rabbit that Rom had caught in a snare during the night, and some bread made from ground acorns. It was a meager meal for seven people so the children were anxious to gather berries. After every scrap of the rabbit was devoured, Oogay motioned for the boys to come closer. Margaret followed behind the boys.

Oogay gave the children a stern look and began to speak. "Rom and I are taking Frik and Frak back to a woodchuck den that we passed on our morning walk. If the dogs can dig Woodchuck out of his house, he will be our supper. Stink will stay with Ma and Gam, so there will be no dogs with you. Keep a sharp eye for danger and don't wander too far. Do you understand?"

"Yes, Da," said Tur.

"Yeff, Da," said Mutt.

"What about you, little chokecherry?" Oogay asked Margaret. It was the first time Oogay had ever spoken directly to Margaret.

"Ya -yes, Da," she stammered.

Oogay broke into a wide grin and said, "Good girl." He bent over to kiss Margaret on the top of the head, turned and whistled for the dogs, then strode away.

CHAPTER 6
MASTODON

It was not easy work picking the black raspberries. The ripe berries hung from thorn covered vines. Before long the children's hands and arms were covered with itchy scratches. The blossoms that would become new berries attracted bees and wasps who would sting if you got too close. Still, the children were able to fill one of Gam's grass baskets with berries.

While picking, Mutt ate so many of the sweet berries that he got a stomach ache and threw up. "Serves you right for being so greedy," Tur scolded.

Margaret took pity on the younger boy. "Tur, let's sit awhile until Mutt feels better."

"Please," whined Mutt.

Tur sighed and sat down next to his brother. There was wood sorrel growing all around them so Tur pulled up a plant and held one out to Mutt. "Chew this, it'll make your stomach feel better." Then he pulled another for Margaret. "Chew the root, it's sour but nice."

Margaret bit off a small piece of the root and began to chew. *It tastes like a lemon sourball,* she decided. For the first time in forever, Margaret felt like she was having fun!

The summer afternoon sky was filled with wisps of clouds and the children stretched out on the ground to watch them go by.

"I see a big fish," said Margaret.

"I see an osprey swooping down to catch your fish," Tur replied. His fingers touched hers. Margaret did not pull her hand away.

"I'm bored," said Mutt. "Let's go." The little boy jumped up and headed back the way they'd come.

On the return trip they strayed from the big trees that lined the river. The upland was drier and the trees were shorter, mostly spruce. There was a lot of open pasture. While they were crossing a small meadow, Tur noticed a male robin flying in and out from the same spot in the upper branches of a leafy silver tree. On the way in the robin had a bug or worm in his beak but on the way out his beak was empty. He was feeding somebody.

Silver beech trees were the best climbing trees so in no time Tur, Margaret, and Mutt were sitting next to each other on a high branch, staring at a mother robin sitting motionless in her nest. Tur stretched a hand toward the nest and the mother robin flew off with a distressed chirp. She had been sitting on a clutch of four blue eggs.

Tur removed three of the eggs. He did not touch the fourth egg because Gam said it was bad medicine to take every egg from a nest. Tur handed the first egg to Mutt, who immediately popped the tiny treat into his mouth and began chewing noisily. Tur held out the second egg to Margaret. "Try it, you'll like it," he said. Margaret shyly accepted Tur's offering with two fingers, placed it between her back teeth and crushed the shell with a single bite. The taste was strong and warm and eggy. By the time Margaret finished chewing her egg, Tur had gobbled the third and was making his way down through the branches. Margaret and Mutt followed.

As the children reached the lowest branch and gathered themselves to jump to the ground, a stand of spruce trees on the far side of the meadow exploded with a crash. Into the grassy clearing spilled two almost-grown bull mastodons. Their heads and backs were flatter than an elephant's, their ears were smaller but their twisted tusks were longer. Both animals were covered with a coat of long, grey hair. *They're almost as big as Old Doc*, thought Margaret.

The young males seemed to be playing and fighting at the same time. They would run together, lock tusks for a moment, then pull apart. Their jousting was accompanied by throaty huffing and loud whistling. Occasionally one would slow down just long enough to pick up a stick or clod of dirt with his trunk and hurl it at the other.

As the two young bulls wrestled, three more mastodons cautiously stepped into the clearing. Two were adult cows and the third was a young female. The grown-ups were slightly taller than the rambunctious bulls but the youngster was only half as big as the males. No adult bull was in the small herd. One of the cows began to strip leaves from bushes that dotted the meadow. Every few minutes she would crush a fan of leaves into a sticky ball with the end of her trunk and pop the green wad into her mouth. While she chewed she kept a watchful eye on the young bulls.

The bulls became more aggressive toward each other so the cows began to back away. The young female was busy trying to uproot a sassafras sapling and not paying attention. One of the bulls backed into her and accidently stomped on one of her rear legs. The children in the beech tree could hear the bone crack as the young mastodon bleated in pain and collapsed.

The cows immediately went to the aid of the injured youngster, stroking her head and neck with their trunks while making throaty sounds of encouragement. Eventually the crippled mastodon stood up but she put no weight on her injured leg.

The young bulls lost interest in their mock battle and the herd began to move back into the spruces. The injured female struggled to keep up.

Mutt started to swing to the ground but Tur grabbed Mutt's hair and yanked him back into the beech. The younger boy's cry of surprise was stifled when Tur clamped his other hand over Mutt's mouth. Tur let go of Mutt's hair and pointed into the clearing.

Two smilodons were crawling on their bellies toward the departing mastodons. The big cats had muscular necks, powerful front shoulders, smaller hind legs and stubby tails. "They're bigger than mountain lions!" whispered Margaret. Tur put a finger to his lips so she stopped talking.

The smilodons had dense coats of striped orange fur. Each had two fangs protruding downward from their upper jaw like daggers. One smilodon was slightly bigger than the other, and the smaller one showed the swollen teats of a nursing mother.

The wind was blowing away from the smilodons and toward the beech tree, so the cats had not picked up the scent of the children. Still, Margaret's heart was beating so fast it seemed about to burst. Her palms were clammy and sweat was running down between her shoulder blades. When Tur and Mutt started a slow climb back up the tree, Margaret was glad to follow.

The trio was halfway up to the branch with the robin's nest when the smilodons rushed forward into the spruce trees. The throaty roars of the attacking cats mixed with the terrified trumpeting of the surprised mastodons. The young bulls and the two cows came crashing back into the meadow and galloped past the beech tree and away into dense brush. The injured youngster was not with them.

When the last fleeing mastodon disappeared from sight, Margaret found herself clinging to a small branch above the robin's nest. From her perch she could see over the spruce trees. The young mastodon with the injured leg was lying motionless on its side in tall grass, and the smilodons were chewing on her belly. Tur shinnied up next to Margaret and put his arm around her shoulders.

"Is the baby dead?" Margaret asked Tur. She began to sniffle and rub her eyes. Tur was perplexed by Margaret's tears.

"Of course it's dead," Tur replied. "Two lions cannot eat an entire mastodon, even a young one. With luck we'll get what the lions leave behind."

The smilodons ate for half an hour. The female managed to chew a large piece of muscle and hide from the rump of the dead mastodon. Holding her prize firmly in her mighty jaws, she padded away into the woods. The male watched her go, then stood and began digging at the ground. He kicked sand and grass over the mastodon carcass. Then he stood stiff and peed on his kill. The strong scent of urine reached the children in the tree.

"Ick," sniffed Margaret. Mutt began to giggle but stopped when Tur threw a twig at him. Smilodons were not good tree climbers but it made no sense to let the big lion know he was being watched.

The male smilodon walked once around the dead mastodon, lifted his head to give a mighty roar, then trotted off in pursuit of his mate.

* * * * *

Once Tur was convinced that the lion was gone, he jumped to the ground and began running toward camp. Margaret and Mutt followed. They arrived out of breath, hands on knees, hardly able to talk.

Rom was skinning two woodchucks for supper. Oogay was tying a new point on the end of his favorite spear. Tana was getting a cooking fire ready and Gam was minding the baby. The three dogs were fighting over a pile of woodchuck guts.

"Did you three see a ghost?" kidded Rom.

"No," gasped Tur, "a lion."

Oogay jabbed the shaft of his spear into the ground, walked over to Tur, and crouched so they were eye to eye. "An adult lion?" he asked his son.

"Yes, Da, two of them. They killed a mastodon but only ate a little before leaving. There's a lot of meat still on the ground."

Oogay looked at Margaret and Mutt. They shook their heads in agreement.

Oogay stood and walked over to Rom for a private conversation. After a few minutes Oogay turned and motioned for everyone to gather around him.

"We must work fast if we are going to steal the lions' kill. We'll take a large bag of cutting stones, our sharpest spears, and all of the rope. We must take what we can before the sun sets. Lions like to return to their kill at night."

Like firemen responding to a four alarm blaze, the family scooped up their tools and began jogging to where the children had seen the lions. Tur led the way, the dogs running with him. They seemed to know something big was about to happen.

The family stopped short of the meadow where the dead mastodon still lay. The carcass was already covered with a half dozen turkey vultures. Their heads were buried in the stomach cavity that had been ripped open by the lions. There was much hissing as the big birds competed for the choice liver and kidneys.

Oogay and Rom carefully circled the meadow looking for lion tracks. They found the tracks where the lions had left the meadow but no new tracks to show they had returned. Convinced that the family was in no immediate danger, the two men threw stones at the vultures to scare them away, then motioned for the others to join them.

"Be as quiet as you can," ordered Oogay. "Margaret, I want you to take the baby and climb up in the same tree where you hid from the lions. Don't climb down until Rom comes for you. And keep your eyes open for lions. Can you whistle?"

Margaret put her fingers in her mouth and made a loud whistle.

"Good girl. Take the baby and go." Tana tied the baby to Margaret using Margaret's old pajama bottoms for a sling. Tana kissed the baby, then turned and stood next to Rom. Margaret jogged to the beech tree and began climbing.

Oogay gave more orders. "Gam, you and Mutt cut green poles and lash them to the dogs. The dogs will carry most of the meat. Rom and Tana, cut off the head. Tur and I will cut up the large hindquarter that the lions left in one piece."

The family set to work as ordered. It took Oogay and Tur less than a half hour to cut two large pieces of meat from the mastodon's right hip. Rom and Tana's task of removing the head was trickier because the neck bones proved hard to cut. Oogay told Mutt to help Tur load the hip meat behind Frik and Frak. Then he went to help Rom and Tana sever the head. Little Stink, with help from the boys, would drag the head.

In about an hour everything was loaded on the dogs. Rom ran over to the beech tree and called for Margaret to come down.

"I'm afraid I'll drop the baby," confessed Margaret. Rom did not criticize her but climbed up into the tree like Tarzan and took the baby. "Climb on to my back," he told Margaret. She held on like a monkey and in the blink of an eye they were on the ground and back with the others. Quietly, the family lined up like camels and started back to camp.

CHAPTER 7
SMILODON

The family worked through the night to butcher and smoke the mastodon meat. They built three fires, two for light to work by and one for cooking and smoking. Using sharp cutters made from chert, Oogay and Rom sliced the hip roasts into long strips for smoking over the biggest fire. Little scraps were turned over to Gam. She grilled the scraps over one end of the big fire until they were crisp like bacon. Later, Gam and Tana would crumble the cooked meat and roll it into balls with woodchuck fat and wild onions. The meatballs would be eaten when the family was on the move and there was no time to cook fresh meat.

Tana and Tur cut the mastodon's tongue out of the head. The tongue weighed over twenty pounds and was covered with tough skin. They laid the tongue on the ground and skinned it. Next, they laid the meat on flat rocks and began sawing it into slices the size of large pork chops. Tana reminded Tur, "Be very careful. If you slip you could cut off a finger."

Mutt, whose job it was to keep the fires blazing with fresh firewood, started to sing, "Fingers and toes, where did they go? Nobody knows."

"Shut up, runt," warned Tur.

Mutt made a face at Tur but stopped singing. He continued to hum.

Margaret minded the baby until it began to fuss.

"Somebody's hungry," said Tana. "Please give her to me."

Margaret was secretly glad to be done babysitting. She handed the baby to Tana and went to watch Tur cutting up the last of the tongue. Tur was on his knees, hunched over and sweating from his effort.

"May I help?" Margaret asked.

Tur did not look up from his work as he answered, "Yes, but be careful. Like Ma said, you can lose a finger if you don't pay attention."

Margaret sat down in order to hold one end of the tongue and make it easier for Tur to cut. Suddenly Tur screamed, "Ow, ow!" and jumped up. A chunk of flesh about the size and shape of a boy's finger dropped into Margaret's lap. She recoiled in horror before realizing it was only a piece of tongue that Tur had carved to look like a finger.

Tur and Mutt rolled around on the ground laughing hysterically and holding their sides.

"That's not nice, Tur, not nice at all!" cried Margaret. To Tur's surprise, Margaret had tears rolling down her cheeks. He began to say "I'm sorry" but Margaret moved away and sat down next to Tana.

"Nephew, you have a lot to learn about girls!" Rom called out from behind the smoking fire. Then it was Rom and Oogay's turn to laugh.

* * * * *

When Margaret woke up the next morning, Oogay and Rom were gone. Frik and Frak were nowhere to be seen. What had been left of the mastodon head was also missing.

"Where are the men?" Margaret asked Gam.

"They've been gone since sunup, sleepyhead," Gam replied. "By tonight we'll be done smoking the mastodon rump and the tongue but we don't have time to deal with the head right now. Oogay knows of a deep spot in the river. He and Rom will weight the head down with rocks and lower it into the deep water. Except for a few hungry turtles, nothing will bother the head while we go on to the Gathering. If we come back this way, the head can be pulled up and I'll make jelly out of the brains."

"Won't the head rot while we are gone?

"Not much. The river spirits keep meat fresh if it's stored in cold, dark water."

Tur and Mutt appeared with armloads of firewood. They had tied extra pieces to Stink's back. The little dog did not look happy about it. The boys began feeding the smoking fire, which was encircled by green poles covered with mastodon jerky.

Tana was sitting on a nearby log, trying to fix a hole in a pair of Oogay's moccasins with a bone needle and some thread made from mastodon gut. The baby was sleeping next to Tana in her basket.

"Don't pile on too much wood," warned Tana. "We want a slow burn with lots of smoke."

Tur obeyed his mother. The poles and strips of meat almost disappeared in a cloud of white smoke. His mother looked pleased so he asked, "Can Mutt and I take a walk to practice throwing our short spears?"

"OK, but don't use poor Stink as a target. I'm through sewing up his cuts and scratches. In fact, let him stay here with Margaret."

The boys untied Stink's bundle of sticks and he immediately ran to Margaret for a scratching behind the ear. Tur and Mutt collected their short spears and loped into the shadows.

* * * * *

At about the same time Oogay and Rom were sinking the mastodon head in the river, the male smilodon returned to his kill. Something was not right! The head was missing and a large piece of the rump was gone. There were many tracks in the soil around the carcass. The lion bent his massive head and sniffed. *Man!* The thought of a man invading his turf and stealing his food made the big cat furious. He paced around the dead mastodon three times, lifted his head and roared a mighty roar. *Thief, I'm coming for you!* The smilodon took off at a trot toward the Oogay family, his huge fangs shining in the sun.

* * * * *

One moment Stink was snoring in Margaret's lap, the next he was up and snarling at an unseen danger. Very quietly Gam said, "Margaret, take that dog with you and go climb the nearest big tree. Tana and I will be right behind you." Margaret quickly did as she was told, found a white pine with low branches and began to climb. Stink remained on the ground, growling at what he knew was coming.

It was the smilodon. The big lion slowly walked into the campsite, his nose filling with the smell of wood smoke and greasy meat. He found the family's bundles of clothes and tools and knocked them about with his giant paws like a house cat playing with a ball of string. He paced back and forth and found the bloody places where the mastodon meat had been cut up during the night. He growled and kicked dirt on the bloody ground.

Gam and Tana and the baby were not able to reach Margaret's pine tree. Instead they squeezed under three dead tree trunks that had fallen into a pile during a storm. It would be difficult for the smilodon to dig them out, but not impossible.

If they remained very quiet the lion might not notice them.

The baby began to cry.

"Rurarrrr?," growled the big cat as he turned toward the sound of the man-child. He began to stalk the crying, head down between his shoulders and his stubby tail shaking ever so slightly.

I must do something to distract the smilodon! thought Margaret. On a branch next to her face were three old pine cones that had been left behind by a squirrel. She grabbed one and threw it as hard as she could at the smilodon. She missed. She tried again and missed again. She held the last cone to her lips, spit on it for luck, and heaved.

The last pinecone hit the smilodon smack in the middle of his butt. He jumped straight up and twisted completely around. He raised his head and peered directly at Margaret. He charged the pine tree and leapt straight up, almost touching Margaret's bare feet with his sharp claws. Margaret screamed and tried to climb higher.

The lion gathered himself to jump again. This time he would use his hind claws to push. He knew he could reach the screaming girl.

Before the smilodon could spring, a snarling fur ball rocketed out of the bushes and onto the lion's back. It was Stink. The little dog bit down as hard as he could.

The lion, enraged, twirled round and round in an attempt to shake off his attacker. Stink, growling as loud as he could with a mouth full of lion hair, hung on for dear life.

The lion's contortions became so furious that he was able to knock Stink off his neck with one of his hind paws. Before Stink could recover the lion had the little dog in his mouth. The huge cat bit down hard, then spit Stink away with a fierce shake of the head. Stink bounced into a pile of leaves and did not move.

The smilodon stood with his legs set far apart, breathing heavily from the exertion of throwing off the dog. He looked up at Margaret, then toward the sound of the crying baby, deciding which one to kill first.

A short spear came sailing out of far bushes and scraped the lion across the top of his shoulders. It made a shallow cut but did not stick. A second short spear followed but the lion ducked and it flew harmlessly by. Tur stepped out from behind the bushes to throw his final spear.

The lion was bewildered. The whole forest seemed to be fighting back. New anger welled up inside him. *I am king of this place, and I do as I will!* He stood up on his hind legs, pawed the air and roared.

He stood up on his hind legs, pawed the air and roared.

That was when a long spear came hurtling from the direction of the river and pierced the smilodon's neck. Bright red blood began to gush down the front of the lion's chest.

"Aaaighhhii!" someone screamed. It was Oogay, running at full speed toward the lion with a stone knife in one hand and a stick in the other. He slid under the smilodon like a baseball player stealing home, wedging the stick in the lion's open mouth to prevent him from closing his jaws.

Wounded and terrified, the lion dug at Oogay with his front claws, cutting big gashes in the top of the man's head. Oogay ducked to protect his eyes, all the while stabbing upward with his knife. There was blood everywhere, partly from Oogay's torn scalp and partly from the wounded smilodon. Oogay couldn't breathe from the weight of the lion pressing down on him. He started to pass out.

Frik and Frak saved Oogay by barreling into the lion and knocking him off their master. The lion managed to smack both dogs away, but as he did so he raised his head and exposed his throat.

Rom, who had sprinted up from the river to help Oogay, saw his opportunity and with a slash of his spear opened the cat's throat, cutting the windpipe. The smilodon made a last futile lunge at Rom and collapsed dead.

* * * * *

Everyone was exhausted and subdued from the fight with the smilodon. Tana and Gam helped Oogay down to the river where they washed away the grime, blood and lion fur that was stuck to his wounds. With their help he slowly walked back to camp and sat next to the only fire that was still burning. Oogay had two deep gashes in his scalp, which Gam sewed together. As a finishing touch she slathered pine pitch over the stitches to keep away biting flies.

As she worked Gam told Tur and Margaret to collect "handfuls of fresh birch bark." The children did as they were told and soon returned with the bark. Gam scraped the green inner bark from the white outer layer, then rolled the green stuff between her hands until it was soft.

"Put this in your mouth and chew slowly," Gam told Oogay. "It will help with the pain." Oogay silently obeyed. He closed his eyes and lay back with his head in Tana's lap. Tana stroked the side of her husband's face and whispered, "My man, my brave man, you saved our children, I love you."

While Gam and Margaret collected the things that had been thrown about the camp by the smilodon, Rom and Tur set to work skinning the huge cat. The lion was too big to move so they cut off his pelt where he lay, taking only the fur from the top of the head, the shoulders and back, and the front legs.

"Gam says it was your spear that killed the lion so you get to keep the fur," Tur said to his uncle. "Will you wear it at the Gathering?"

"No," replied Rom, "I have something else in mind."

After they were done removing the lion's pelt and had stretched it over a frame of sticks, Rom said to Tur, "Did you bring a short spear like I asked you?"

"Yes, uncle."

"Give it to me."

Tur handed over the spear. Rom jammed the point in the smilodon's upper jaw, above one of the lion's saber teeth, and rocked the spear back and forth until the big tooth came free. Rom rolled the head over and removed the other long tooth in the same way. He picked up the teeth and handed them to Tur. "A boy who is brave enough to throw a spear at a lion is no longer a boy. Wear these like a man." Tur beamed as they walked back to camp with the fangs.

At the end of the fight with the lion, Mutt had run to Stink's side and discovered the dog was dead. He would not let anyone else touch Stink and carried the little dog back to camp by himself. Mutt spent the afternoon sitting alone, hugging Stink, tears running down his face.

Mutt fell asleep holding Stink's lifeless body. After several hours he awoke to find Oogay standing over him.

"Little man, time to give Stink a warrior's funeral, don't you think?"

Mutt shook his head "Yes" and fresh tears began to fall. Oogay slowly scooped up the boy and dead dog and headed down to the river.

Rom and Tur were standing next to a tiny bier of long grass balanced on a pile of firewood. Tana and Margaret had decorated the little bed with blue lupine blooms.

Oogay bent over the bier and Mutt dropped Stink's body into the little bed. He continued to hold his da around the neck as Oogay stepped back so Rom could light the fire.

"Great Spirit of the north," Gam chanted, "this dog has a small body but a big heart. Take him to your home beyond the Big Ice so he might play with all the other brave dogs who have gone before him."

As the flames climbed to surround the bier, the family turned away and headed back to camp. They would not need to hunt meat or fish for a week and would be on time for the Gathering.

PART II

THE GATHERING

CHAPTER 8
CHERT

Oogay's family arrived at the Gathering two days later. The Gathering reminded Margaret of the state park campground back home. In the center there were two lodges, one for the men and one for the women, made of green poles covered with hides. The individual family campsites were scattered in a wide ring around the lodges. Each of the four clans was represented by five to ten families, and those families camped next to each other.

It was mid-morning when Oogay's family found a level place to pitch their lean-to and stash their belongings. While the others unpacked, Gam headed for the women's lodge. She called back over her shoulder, "Margaret, come with me."

It was a short walk to the lodges. Margaret was impressed by the immense mammoth tusks that framed the door flaps of both lodges. Each tusk was taller than a man. When she and Gam arrived there was a wooden staff decorated with three mammoth teeth leaning against the doorway of the women's lodge. It was a signal that only women old enough to have children and grandchildren were allowed to enter that morning.

"Stay here," said Gam. She pulled back the flap and stepped inside.

Margaret could hear laughter and cries of welcome. She tiptoed around the outer wall of the lodge until she found a small tear in one of the hides. She kneeled and put her eye to the opening.

Eight old women were standing and taking turns giving Gam a hug. When the hugging was finished they sat down to share the news of happy times and sad times that had taken place since the last Gathering. Gam spoke last.

"Our family found a lost little girl. Her ma is dead. She says her da's name is 'Joe.' I thought he might come to the Gathering to look for his daughter. Have any of you heard of a man with that odd name?" There were murmurs and shakes of the head. Nobody had seen or heard of "Joe."

"I hear people saying the girl is not of our people," croaked the oldest of the women. "She's pale as a ghost and her hair's the color of dandelion tops. What if she brings bad luck? Are you sure she should be here?"

Gam raised her chin and said, "Margaret, come inside. I know you're listening." Margaret was embarrassed at having been caught eavesdropping but she did as Gam commanded.

When Margaret entered the lodge Gam took her by the arm and led her to the center. "When someone asks you a question, look at them when you answer," Gam whispered. "Be friendly, but act confident."

The oldest woman squinted at Margaret and asked the first questions. "Where do you come from? Does everyone in your clan have yellow hair?"

Remembering Gam's advice, Margaret looked straight into the eyes of the old woman and replied, "My da told me that my ma had yellow hair. My da has dark hair like yours. I come from far away and am lost.

"Can you read signs and make spells?" asked another old lady.

"No, I don't think so."

"I will teach her," Gam interrupted.

"Let me see your teeth," demanded another woman.

"Go ahead, Margaret, open your mouth," said Gam.

Margaret opened wide and each old lady took a turn peering into Margaret's mouth. Everyone agreed that Margaret had the whitest teeth they'd ever seen.

The oldest woman spoke again. "I have decided this girl is not an evil spirit. Her skin may be oddly white and her hair mysteriously yellow, but a person should not be judged by how she looks. Besides, I wish I had Margaret's beautiful teeth!" The old lady grinned so Margaret could see she only had three teeth left in her mouth.

The conversation returned to who had died since the last Gathering, who had new grandchildren, and who had daughters and granddaughters of marrying age. Margaret listened quietly and began to realize that across the clans women had the last word in family matters. When a man married he became a member of his wife's family and clan. An old widow lived with her daughters. If she had no daughters, she could live with a son if the daughter-in-law gave her permission.

When the sun reached its highest point in the sky, the meeting broke up. On the stroll back to Oogay's campsite Margaret asked, "Gam, what if I don't find my da?"

Gam stopped and took Margaret's hands in hers. "In that case, my little yellow hair, Tana and I want you to become part of our family. What do you say to that?"

"I say yes!" For the first time since being dragged under water by the giant catfish, Margaret didn't feel lost.

* * * * *

While Margaret and Gam were at the women's lodge, Oogay and Rom climbed to a high banks area above the river. Long ago the river had flowed along the top of the high banks. Over many years the river's current had cut through the soft rock and the river had fallen.

The face of the high banks was crumbly limestone. Scattered through the limestone, and far below along the river bank, were many round rocks. The rocks varied in size between a golf ball and a grapefruit.

The round rocks were made of chert. If a chert ball was hammered with a small fieldstone, a sharp wedge of the chert ball would split off. The edges of the chert wedge could be pounded with the butt end of an antler, or a piece of mammoth ivory, to make the wedge thinner and sharper. Finally, the pointy end of an antler could be used to chip small flakes from the edge of the thin wedge. The result was a very sharp tool.

The men of the four clans knew how to make a variety of tools from chert, including spear points, knives, cutting tools and scraping tools. The tools became dull or broken with use, so every family needed a good supply of spare chert tools to last a year until the next Gathering.

The men worked in teams. Rom joined a team that was collecting chert rocks from along the river bank and prying chert from the softer limestone layers. The rocks were piled next to a second team. That team clubbed the round rocks into big wedges and then thinner wedges. Oogay had good eyesight for close work, so he joined a third team that was in charge of the finish flaking. When a tool was finished it was placed into a basket with other tools of the same kind. There were baskets for large and small spear points, baskets for knives and scrapers, and a basket for axe heads. The men would work together every morning for two weeks. When the gathering was over, each family would take away a share of the new tools.

Some chert was not worked into tools but set aside in wedge shaped chunks. Those wedges of chert would be traded to Indians who were not of the four clans. The men of the Lion Clan were especially keen to trade chert. After the Gathering, some of them would travel farther to the east to trade chert for salt or caribou hides.

As the heat of mid-day arrived, the men stopped working the chert and headed back to their campsites for a meal. As Oogay and Rom walked along, Rom began to nervously ask him questions.

"Have you ever gone east to trade chert?"

"I thought about it before I married Tana, but my mother's clan was Beaver and they were fond of hunting, not trading," Oogay replied.

"I might tag along with men of the Lion Clan when they go trading this year."

Oogay stopped, cocked his head at Rom, and said, "Is that so?"

"Not if it causes a problem for the family!" Rom's voice cracked and he began to sweat. "I would never do that."

Oogay put a hand on the top of Rom's shoulder. "You have been a good teacher to Tur. He listens to you. For that I will always be grateful. Every man must make his own way. You go with the men of the Lion Clan, if they'll have you. Tur and I will hunt and fish while you are gone. The family will be fine. Now, let's go see what your sister has made for us to eat."

CHAPTER 9
PODI

The family enjoyed roasted white suckers for lunch, which they ate while lounging in the shade of a big boxelder. As Tana handed out portions she cleared her throat and said, "I saw Podi at the river flats this morning. She'd trapped a large basket of fish and asked me to take some for lunch."

Oogay, his mouth full of fish, mumbled, "I've always liked that girl. Remember how last year she and Rom ran around camp for hours playing tag with Mutt?"

"I was not playing tag with Podi!" Rom protested. "Her little brother liked to play with Mutt and she was babysitting her brother. I only kept her company to pass the time."

"Is she still scrawny and knock-kneed?" teased Oogay.

Rom swallowed the last of his lunch and frowned at his brother-in-law.

"Not at all," Tana answered. "She's taller, and she is rounder where a woman should be round." Tana bent down by her younger brother's ear and whispered, "She'll make somebody a good wife. I wonder who?"

Rom stood up and announced, "I've got better things to do than sit here and gossip." He picked up his shoulder bag and marched off.

When Rom was out of earshot Gam scolded, "Why do you two torture that boy? I hope he doesn't lose his nerve."

"No chance of that happening," laughed Oogay. "Rom won't quit, he's stubborn like his big sister."

"Very funny," said Tana, and she threw the last sucker at Oogay's head. He ducked and the fish landed in tall weeds. Frik pounced on the treat and wolfed it down while Frak watched and whined.

"Da," asked Mutt, "can I go after Rom? I want to say hello to Podi's brother."

Oogay looked at Tana. She nodded "yes."

"Alright," Oogay decided, "but only if Tur and Margaret go with you."

"Oh, great," muttered Tur.

"I think it'll be fun," Margaret offered. "I want to meet this Podi person."

Gam stood up and stretched. "If you two don't mind," she said to Tana and Oogay, "while the children are gone I'm going to visit an old friend in the Caribou Clan and show her the baby." Gam gathered the baby's things, picked up the baby, and left. A few moments later Tur, Mutt, and Margaret took off to find Rom.

Oogay winked at Tana as he waved goodbye to the children with the back of his hand. "I think Podi's clan is camped over there somewhere. Don't hurry back, your Ma and I want to take an afternoon nap."

* * * * *

Rom was not happy to have Tur, Margaret, and Mutt tag along but he maintained his composure and did his best to appear indifferent to their company. He walked with head high and shoulders back, trying to make himself look older. He headed to the camps of the Lion Clan.

A young woman could marry outside of her clan so long as her parents agreed. A big show was always made of asking a father's permission to court his daughter, but everybody knew that it was the young woman's mother and grandmothers and aunts who had the last word.

Rom found Podi sitting inside a lean-to with her mother and aunt. Tana had not lied, Podi was indeed taller and . . . rounder. She was so beautiful it made Rom weak in the knees.

When Podi noticed Rom she smiled and waved but said nothing. She nodded toward the front of the lean-to. There, much to Rom's dismay, was a line of three suitors waiting to speak with Podi's father. He was a heavy set, stern looking fellow, adorned with a necklace of smilodon claws and sitting on a makeshift throne of firewood.

Podi leaned close to her mother and whispered, "See, I told you Rom would come! Doesn't he look handsome?"

"He's not yet full grown," Podi's mother decided. "I doubt he owns anything but his spear and the clothes on his back. Still, if he lifts your heart I will not object. I know his sister Tana and she is a good person."

"Thank you, Ma!" Podi hugged her mother.

"Well, better hope your young man makes a good impression with your father. We want Da to think the match is his idea."

Rom got into line with his brothers and Margaret trailing behind. He turned and quietly said, "You three keep still and say nothing. If you behave I'll find us some sweet prickly pear for a treat." Mutt began to holler for joy but Tur shut him up with a hand over the mouth.

One at a time the suitors introduced themselves, announced their intention to court Podi, and laid a gift on the ground for her father's consideration.

The first two suitors were older members of the Lion Clan who had hunted with Podi's father. One offered a long spear adorned with feathers and charms. The other presented a lap blanket made from the skin of a bear cub. Podi's father looked unimpressed but politely thanked them for their gifts.

The third suitor appeared to be Rom's age. From the back of the line Margaret observed, *He's the tallest person I've seen at the Gathering, and he's only a teenager.*

The tall young man announced, "My name is Bo." Rom could tell Bo was from the Beaver Clan because Bo's moccasins were trimmed in beaver fur. Like Rom, Bo was carrying a shoulder bag. But Bo's bag was squirming.

"I raise dogs," Bo began. "I bring you the pick of this year's litter. He's smart and brave and will be a great hunter, like Podi's father." Bo opened his bag and a white and brown pup jumped to the ground, tail wagging.

Mutt could not help himself. He squealed "Puppy!" and ran toward the dog. Instead of shying away the puppy jumped into Mutt's arms and began to lick his face.

"Don't you teach your dogs to heel?" asked Podi's father. He did not thank Bo for the gift but said, "I don't need another dog." Bo's face turned deep red. He said nothing and yanked the puppy away from Mutt.

Finally it was Rom's turn. Although he and Podi had spent time together at last year's gathering, Rom had never spoken with her father before.

"I am Rom of the Mammoth Clan, son of Gam and brother of Tana. Podi and I played together as children. Now I wish to spend time with her as a man."

Podi's father stared at Rom and said nothing.

Rom wet his lips with his tongue and continued. "On our way to the Gathering my family was attacked by a lion. I helped kill it to protect those I love. I will always protect your daughter."

With that Rom lifted the orange smilodon pelt from his shoulder bag and stretched it out on the ground before Podi's father. There was a murmur from the crowd. It was obvious from the size of the skin that it had been a very big lion.

Podi father stood and held up the lion pelt for all to see, then turned and handed it to Podi's mother. He turned back to Rom and said, "I know," touching the claws around his neck, "it is not easy to kill a lion. You may spend time with my daughter."

With that Podi leapt to her feet and ran to stand next to Rom. She took Rom's hand before her father could change his mind. The young couple smiled at each other and strolled away.

Podi's father thanked all for coming and ducked into the lean-to. "Was that alright?" he asked his wife.

"You were perfect," replied Podi's mother, and kissed him on the cheek.

* * * * *

Bo was furious. It was bad enough that Podi obviously preferred that idiot from the Mammoth Clan, but her father's rejection of Bo's gift was a shame he would never forget.

"Dog-man, mister dog-man, please wait!" Mutt had run after Bo and his yelling made the big teenager stop and turn.

"What do you want, pest?" snarled Bo.

"I want to buy your puppy," squeaked Mutt. Tur and Margaret jogged up and stood behind Mutt.

"Oh, is that so?" said Bo. "What do you have to trade?"

Mutt dug under the waistband of his loincloth and produced three Petoskey stones, plus the shiny water beetle that he gotten from Margaret.

"That's little kid junk," Bo sneered. "Don't waste my time."

Mutt looked like he might cry.

"That jerk who claims he killed a lion, what's he to you?"

"My uncle," sniffled Mutt.

"Is that so? I bet he's a liar."

"He's no liar," said Tur, stepping forward with clenched fists.

Bo laughed at Tur. "Save it, shorty. I don't fight with children." Bo picked up the pup and held it out at arm's length, making the little animal whine in fear. "You know, this may not be such a good dog after all. He's nice and fat, though. I think I'll take him back to camp and cook him for supper."

"No!" wailed Mutt. The little boy grabbed Tur around the waist and pleaded, "Tur, don't let him eat my dog."

Bo put the pup under his arm and began to walk away.

"Wait," Tur called, "would you take this for the dog?" He removed his necklace of the two smilodon fangs and held it up for Bo to see.

Bo took the necklace and lightly ran a finger along the razor sharp edge of one tooth.

"Where did you get this?"

"My uncle gave it to me when he skinned the lion."

"Oh, really? Well, it's mine now." Bo put the necklace around his neck and took a step.

Margaret ran around Bo and stood defiantly in his way.

"Do we have a deal or not? If you take that necklace *and* the dog, I'll tell every girl at the Gathering that you steal from children. Just try to get a woman interested in you then!" Margaret's eyes were blazing.

Bo was not sure what to do. He stared at the pale little girl for a moment, then dropped the pup at her feet.

"Here, take the crummy pup. I don't like the taste of dog anyway." He stomped off in a huff.

Mutt fell on the pup and they happily became a single squirming ball, giggling and yipping and rolling around on the ground.

"It was kind of you to trade your necklace for the puppy," Margaret told Tur. "Joe – that's my da – says bullies always get what they deserve. But Bo didn't deserve your necklace."

"He's a lot bigger than me so what else could I do? Besides, Mutt needs a dog a lot more than I needed that dumb necklace. Let's get back to camp."

CHAPTER 10
CARIBOU

Not all of the men worked every day to make chert tools. Each morning a few of them would go hunting. Meat brought back from the daily hunt was shared by all of the families at the Gathering.

The morning after Mutt got his new puppy, Oogay and Rom went hunting. They were joined by three of Oogay's friends from the Caribou Clan. Tur and Margaret and Podi followed along. There was no rule against women hunting, so long as they kept up. Each of the older men carried a shoulder bag filled with skinning tools, and a bundle of short spears. Tur carried their big spears.

After walking for an hour the hunters found a fresh game trail winding through stands of spruce and past the occasional leafy tree. Wide hoof prints in the dirt proved that caribou were using the trail. The hunters followed the trail until it passed under a clump of three shagbark hickory trees. Oogay's old friends climbed up into the trees and sat behind green branches. Rom climbed up after them. The four men were hidden but still had room to throw short spears at passing animals.

"Come with me," Oogay said to Podi, Margaret and Tur. They walked up the trail for about ten minutes. A slight breeze was blowing in their faces. When they stopped Oogay reached into his shoulder bag and pulled out two pieces of caribou antler. He gave one to Podi and the other to Margaret.

"Tur and I will go ahead and watch for caribou. When we whistle like a shrike" –Tur gave two short whistles – "you will know caribou are on the trail and coming your way. When that happens, slowly walk back down the trail toward where Rom and the others are hiding in the trees. Every few steps rub a piece of antler against a small spruce or a shrub. Caribou are curious and will follow the noise so long as they don't see you. Don't stop when you reach Rom. Keep going. Do you have questions?"

"How far beyond the men do we go?" asked Margaret.

"Not far. When the men throw their spears your job is over. Don't stray from the game trail. Tur and I don't need any more practice finding lost girls."

Tur snickered. When he turned to follow Oogay back up the trail, Margaret stuck her tongue out at him.

Podi smiled but did not laugh. Instead, she whispered, "Let's hide behind a tree and wait for Tur's whistle."

They did not have to wait long. Two shrill tweets echoed through the trees, which meant the caribou were coming. Podi began to walk down the trail and Margaret followed.

The girls walked a dozen paces before stopping to make a rubbing noise with their antler pieces. Then they walked another ten paces and made more noise. After fifteen minutes they were under the trees where the men were hiding.

"I can see one of Rom's legs and the faces of the others," whispered Margaret.

"It doesn't matter," Podi whispered back, "because caribou don't look up when they walk through the woods."

The girls walked beyond the men hiding in the treetops and dropped behind an ancient pine stump. It was a good hiding place from which to watch the ambush.

Margaret did her best to be quiet, but she could hear her own breathing and feel the pounding of her heart. No wonder men insisted on doing the hunting, it was *exciting*.

A sharp snap broke the silence. Something or somebody had stepped on a dry twig. Margaret held her breath and peeked around the stump.

Coming down the trail were four adult caribou and a calf. One of the adults was a buck and the others were does, but all had magnificent broad antlers. The calf had two antler buttons starting to show on the top of its head.

The animals were dark grey. The buck had a blaze of lighter fur on his throat and chest. The buck's shoulders were as tall as Margaret. The does were slightly shorter. All of the adults were about six feet long from head to tail. *They look like Santa's reindeer*, thought Margaret.

As they walked, the adult caribou grazed on grass and nibbled at the green tips of spruce branches. One of the caribou spooked a blue jay out of a small spruce, and the bird made a loud jeering call as it flew off. The caribou froze. After remaining motionless for several minutes, they began again to walk toward the hiding hunters. The calf and does walked in front while the buck brought up the rear. Each time one of animals lowered its head to graze, it first looked to the right and left. Podi was right - the caribou never looked up, even when walking beneath a clump of hickory trees. It was their big mistake.

The first spear was thrown by Rom and hit one of the does in the spine. She was able to run only a few paces before falling into a heap. The other men threw three more spears. One spear hit another doe in the shoulder and the others missed the buck. The buck made a leaping turn and bolted back up the trail in the direction of Oogay and Tur. The third doe and the calf fled away from the trail, through a thick wall of spruce, and into a clearing on the other side.

The men quickly climbed to the ground to retrieve their spears. Rom finished the doe on the ground with a quick stab to the heart. The doe with the wounded shoulder had limped off, leaving a trail of blood on the forest floor. She could not last long. Two of the men from the Caribou Clan went to find her.

Rom and the other man carried Rom's dead doe to the base of a hickory tree and tied vines around the animal's hind feet. They threw the vines over a sturdy limb and hauled the doe off the ground so it could be easily gutted, skinned and deboned. The man from the Beaver Clan began to butcher the caribou with a sharp piece of chert. Rom walked over to Podi and Margaret.

"Let's see if we can find that last doe and her calf," said Rom. He found their trail and began to jog through the spruce trees and toward the meadow. Podi and Margaret followed.

Rom, Podi, and Margaret emerged from the spruce to a frightening sight. The doe and the calf were surrounded by a circle of dire wolves. It was clear to see that the largest wolf had a white blaze across the left side of his face. "It's the wolves from the river," whispered Margaret.

The wolves took turns rushing at the doe. When she lunged back at the attacker with her antlers, another wolf would lunge at the calf and bite at its hind legs.

"They'll kill the baby!" cried Margaret.

"Shhhhh" whispered Podi, "there's nothing we can do about it. Every animal must eat to live, and wolves eat caribou."

"Podi," Rom said quietly, "take Margaret back to the trail and let the others know about the wolves. I'll follow in a minute. I want to make sure the wolves haven't picked up our scent."

Podi and Margaret walked quickly and quietly back to the trail. Oogay and Tur had arrived, pulling a dead caribou behind them. Oogay had speared the buck as it fled from the ambush. Two hunters from the Beaver Clan had found the wounded doe, dead from loss of blood. Three caribou were hanging beneath the hickory trees, in various stages of being skinned and cut into pieces.

"What's the matter?" asked Oogay. "And where is Rom?"

"Wolves have cornered the last doe and her calf," answered Podi. "Rom sent us to tell you."

Oogay said nothing but picked up his heavy spear and set off at a run, following the tracks made by Podi and Margaret in their retreat back to the trail. He had not gone far into the spruce trees when he met Rom.

"The wolves have killed the calf and are busy eating," said Rom. "They did not catch my scent. We should leave."

As fast as possible the hunting party finishing cutting up the three caribou. Each hide was spread on the ground and meat chunks piled inside. The meat bundles were tied onto the backs of the three men from the Beaver Clan. All the short spears and extra shoulder bags were carried by Tur, Margaret, and Podi. Everyone started back to camp at a quick pace, with Oogay and Rom in the back as a rear guard.

"The biggest wolf had a white streak on his face," Rom told Oogay as they walked.

"So they're the same wolves that killed the beaver at the rapids?"

"I think so. Is it possible they've been following us?"

Oogay was silent for several moments, then replied, "No trips outside of camp for the children unless you or I go along."

That night everyone was glad to receive a share of the caribou meat. There was much talk among the men about the dire wolves. It was decided that sentries with dogs would stand guard through the night. Oogay and Rom volunteered for the first watch.

CHAPTER 11
PASSENGER PIGEONS

On their way back to camp from the chert mine Oogay and Tur watched as a flock of passenger pigeons flew by. There were so many, they blocked the sun as they passed. The birds circled and landed in a stand of oak trees that were clumped together in a far meadow.

"A passenger pigeon is bigger than a mourning dove," Oogay told Tur. "Males and females both have blue wings, blue head, a grey underside, and a soft red breast. They roost in huge flocks. And when one bird gets scared and takes flight, the others always follow. Remember that."

Later, Oogay and Tana were inside their lean-to, watching the daylight fade. They lay on their sides next to each other. Oogay hugged Tana around the waist while she nursed the baby. Speaking in low tones so not to wake Margaret and Gam, Oogay told Tana about the pigeons.

"Every clan has as least one family, like ours, who spends a lot of time fishing," Oogay said. "I think fishing nets would be strong enough to catch pigeons."

"I agree," replied Tana. She sat up to burp the baby. "But men don't like to share their fishing tackle. I'll need your help." Tana explained to Oogay what she wanted him to do.

The next morning Tana led two dozen women and girls out of camp and toward the far oak trees, Podi and Margaret among them. Oogay had convinced the fishermen in camp to give up their nets for a day. Teams of two women each carried long poles between which was tied a fishing net. When the poles were separated the net would stretch out and snare anything that tried to fly through. The pigeon hunters had four such traps.

Six of the younger girls, including Margaret, carried short sticks with a cord tied to the end.

At the end of the cord was a large pine cone.

It took less than an hour to reach the roosting pigeons. As the women approached the oaks they could see that the branches were heavy with birds. The scene reminded Margaret of an apple orchard filled with fruit, except the oaks were taller than fruit trees and each pigeon was much bigger than an apple. About half of the birds were on the ground eating acorns. The rest were happily cooing and warbling in the branches.

The women and girls hid in some nearby spruce. They huddled around Tana for final instructions.

"Those with the traps," Tana began, "will crawl into the open and slowly unwind your nets. Those with the pine cone sticks will stay on the edges. Podi and I will sneak to the other side of the oak trees. When we show ourselves and yell, the birds will panic and take off. If you have a pine cone stick, stand and twirl the pine cone so it makes a buzzing noise. That should make the pigeons fly straight ahead. The rest of you stand and lift the nets as high as you can into the air. With luck each net should fill up with birds."

Tana and Podi disappeared into the brush and began creeping to the far side of the oaks. The women with the nets slowly crawled on their hands and knees toward the roosting pigeons. Margaret and the others tiptoed to the edges of the meadow and stood ready to twirl their buzz sticks.

Before everyone was quite ready, a solitary ground sloth appeared at one edge of the meadow. He rambled toward the middle, sat back on his hind legs, and sniffed the wind.

The ground sloth was a huge shaggy beast, as big as a bear, with a large stubby tail behind his back legs and huge claws on his front paws. He ate plants and would rip a tree to shreds with his claws before putting the tasty parts into his immense mouth.

This sloth seemed to be pondering whether to make a meal from the bark of the oak trees. As the sloth stared their way the pigeons became silent.

Margaret was half hidden in some tall grass at the edge of the meadow. She was down on one knee, using her pine cone stick like a cane to steady herself. Margaret did not know that the sloth was a plant eater, and she was scared that she might be the giant's next meal. "Please, please go away," she whispered.

The sloth had excellent hearing and he turned his head toward Margaret. He made a low "Snurff, snurff," sound deep in his throat, and began to sway his tan colored head back and forth to get a better look at Margaret.

The pigeons took comfort from the sloth's interest in Margaret. They began to cluck and warble again as if the sloth was no bother.

At that instant Tana and Podi leapt from some bushes on the other side of the oak trees, yelling "Fly, fly, fly away!" while frantically waving their arms.

The startled pigeons sprang into the air with a mighty swooshing sound. All of the pine cone girls, except Margaret, stood up and made their sticks buzz like angry bees. As Tana had predicted, the birds turned away from the buzzing noises and flew straight into the middle of the meadow. There the snare teams lifted their nets high into the air. Hundreds of pigeons were snared in the webbing of the nets and fell struggling to the ground.

The sudden commotion made the ground sloth take to his heels. For a giant he was surprisingly fast. In his eagerness to escape the sound of the frantic pigeons, the sloth ran right at the kneeling Margaret. She threw away her pine cone stick and dropped to the ground, curling into a small ball.

The sloth ran over Margaret without stepping on her. His immense front paws struck the earth near the top of Margaret's head and his rear paws came down just beyond her quivering feet. The sloth managed to step on Margaret's pine cone stick, splintering it into toothpicks, before he disappeared at a run into the spruce trees.

It took Margaret a few moments to decide if she was hurt. She felt her arms and legs and neck for cuts and scrapes. She slowly stood up and twisted her head, then her waist, to make sure nothing was broken. "How did that -- whatever it was – not flatten me?" she said to nobody in particular.

"Margaret, are you all right?"

Margaret turned to face Podi. "I think so," she said. "What was that thing?"

"A sloth," Podi answered. "They are bad tempered and usually stand and fight when threatened. You are lucky that one decided to run. I was so scared for you!" Podi wrapped her arms around Margaret and hugged her tight.

"Podi, Margaret," – it was Tana calling – "please come here and help kill these pigeons before they get loose and fly away!" The girls quit hugging and with giggles scampered over to help Tana.

* * * * *

"Just a few more to go, and we'll be done."

The pigeon hunters had caught and killed almost four hundred passenger pigeons. Each family at the Gathering had been given a share of the birds to clean, cook and eat. Oogay and Rom had removed the guts from their share. Gam was in charge of feather plucking, with Tur, Margaret and Mutt as her reluctant helpers. The children were sitting cross-legged on the ground, a woven grass bag of feathers in front of each of them.

"Make sure all of the feathers go in your bags. Even the smallest feather can be useful." Gam scooped up the many feathers that were scattered on the ground around Mutt, but she did not scold the little boy.

This is so boring! thought Margaret. Her fingers were sore from pulling feathers. To liven things up she decided to ask Gam a question.

"Gam, what's the Big Ice?"

"I promised to explain the Big Ice, didn't I?" Gam replied. "Well, long ago the earth was so cold that everything was covered with a sheet of thick ice, many times higher than the tallest tree. There was only ice, no plants, no animals, no people. The North Wind became bored blowing across nothing but ice, so it called out to its brother the Sun: 'Brother, make your fire hotter to melt the ice.' The Sun blazed and the Big Ice began to melt. Where the ice melted the grass began to grow, and then the birch and spruce, and after that the white pine and the big leafy trees. The animals, big and small, came to life and learned to eat the grass and the trees. Some crawled into the rivers and became fish. As time went on some of the animals began to eat meat. Finally, people came to be."

"Is the Big Ice gone?" Margaret asked.

"Oh no, most of it still exists. If a person walks north from this place, for a week, maybe two, she will find the edge of the Big Ice."

"Will the Big Ice ever grow bigger again?"

"Nobody knows, child. Some people think 'yes', others think 'no.'"

"What do you think?"

Gam looked to the sky before answering. "Does it matter? If the spirits become angry they can cover the world in ice and start over. But don't worry – I think the spirits love *you* very much."

CHAPTER 12
RATTLESNAKE

Margaret stood shivering on the shore of the little pond, her deerskin jumper wrapped around her middle like a beach towel. She had untied her long braids so her yellow hair fell in a tangled mess to the small of her back. The pond was filled with women and girls from all of the four clans. The biggest feast of the Gathering was to be held that night, followed by a dance competition. The women would wear their finest dresses and jewelry. Almost all of the women were bathing in the pond. And they were naked!

A few of the women remained on the shore with the babies and toddlers. It would be their turn to wash when the first group was done. Podi was still on the shore, sitting with Tana's baby while Tana and Gam bathed together. "What's the matter, Margaret," called Podi, "is the water too cold for you?"

Margaret turned and smiled weakly at Podi. She turned back to stare at the women and girls in the water, most of whom where pairing off to comb each other's long hair. *I can do this*, thought Margaret, *if they don't care, I don't care*. She took a deep breath, dropped her dress on the grass and ran as fast as she could into the water. Her left foot caught a weed and she tripped and fell under. When she popped up, sputtering, she was standing next to Tana and Gam.

"Nice of you to join us," Gam chuckled. "You've smelled like animal guts since you returned from yesterday's hunt." Before Margaret could object, Tana and Gam were vigorously scrubbing her with small pieces of deer hide.

"Turn around and stand still," ordered Gam. Margaret did as she was told and Gam began to untangle Margaret's hair with a comb made from mammoth ivory. At the same time Tana began combing Gam's hair. *I must admit*, thought Margaret, *this feels nice.*

All of the women seemed to be having a pleasant time, talking and laughing while they washed. Margaret noticed that every woman of the Mammoth Clan, and some of their teenage daughters, had a mammoth tattooed somewhere on their body. Tana's tattoo was on her back below her right shoulder blade. It was bigger than Gam's tattoo but the exact same mammoth design. Others displayed their tattoos on shoulders, arms or hips.

Two girls not much older than Margaret waded through the group carrying baskets filled with wild flowers, berries, tiny pine cones, bits of vine, fresh water clamshells and shiny pebbles. Every woman was free to pick items from the baskets and weave them into their hair.

After a while everyone waded back to shore and sat down to dry in the sunshine. More attention was given to hairstyling. Tana had brought a pouch filled with her favorite hair decorations. She asked Gam to weave several into her long black braids.

While working on Tana's hair, Gam said, "Margaret, how would you like some bluebells tied to your yellow braids? Their season is almost over, but while we were washing I noticed some late blooms on the other side of the pond."

"That would be nice," Margaret answered. "May I gather them?" Margaret was mostly dry and she was anxious to get dressed.

"Go ahead. See that willow tree across the pond?" Margaret squinted at the other side of the pond and nodded her head yes.

"The bluebells are in a sunny spot to the right of the willow. Be careful where you walk because this time of day rattlesnakes like to lie in the sun."

Margaret pulled on her dress and moccasins and began following the edge of the pond around to its far side. Podi was in the pond, washing her hair, and waved to Margaret.

Margaret discovered that hundreds of long branches tumbled down from the crown of the willow tree, and at the base of the tree the ground was shady and cold. A flat sunny spot just beyond the shadow of the willow was filled with pretty blue flowers. Margaret made a pocket out of the hem of her dress to hold the blooms as she stooped and picked.

After a few minutes Margaret decided she had picked enough flowers to decorate her hair, and to share with Podi if the older girl wanted to use them. Margaret stood up, then froze when she heard a terrifying sound.

"Chhhhhhiiiiit, chhhhhhiiiiit, chhhhhhiiiiit!" It was the angry rattle of the biggest snake Margaret had ever seen. The serpent was coiled on top of a large flat rock, its body as big around as a man's forearm. The snake's rattle pointed up from the end of its tail. On the other end was the hissing head. The snake moved its head slowly from side to side, occasionally opening its mouth as a warning. Margaret could see two dripping fangs hanging from the top of the snake's mouth. Margaret was so scared she could not say a word. The snake raised its head to strike.

What happened next took place in the blink of an eye. A long forked stick seemed to appear from thin air and pin the snake's head to the ground. Margaret looked up and realized Podi was wielding the stick. Except for moccasins, Podi was bare naked and water still dripped from her uncombed hair. As the big snake hissed and thrashed about, Podi used her left hand to keep the head pinned with the stick. In Podi's right hand was a long chert knife, which she swung downward in a slashing motion. The snake's head flew away and after a moment of squirming the body went limp. Podi bent over the lifeless body and cut the rattle from the end of the tail. She handed the rattle to the wide-eyed Margaret, saying, "Put this rattle in your hair and you will never be bitten by a snake."

Margaret's mouth was so dry she was barely able to say, "Thank you."

The two friends carried the snake back to where Tana and Gam were waiting. The older women had finished putting on their finest dresses.

"That's a nice snake," pronounced Gam. "Menfolk are better behaved when you feed them rattlesnake. Podi, cook that snake for Rom and I bet he'll make you a beautiful belt from the skin."

"I don't think my brother needs to eat snake meat in order to be nice to Podi," said Tana. That made Margaret and Gam laugh, and Podi blush.

After helping Podi dress and comb out her hair, the little group gathered their things and headed back to camp.

* * * * *

As Gam, Tana, Podi, and Margaret strolled back to camp, they passed a group of men from the Caribou Clan who were lashing immense bison haunches to poles made of green cedar. One of the men trotted over to Gam and spoke with her in private while the others waited. When Gam returned she explained, "While we were bathing that man and his sons tracked down a bison that had been running away from a pack of wolves. When they got close the bison charged and stuck one of the boys with a long horn. The father asked me to sew up the boy's wound before he bleeds to death. I will not be gone long. The feasting and dancing won't begin until dark, so go back and finish making yourselves beautiful."

"Gam. . ." said Margaret.

"Yes, child?

"Did the bison hunter see the wolves that were chasing the bison?"

"Only from far away. He said the biggest wolf had a face that was half white and half black."

Podi headed back to her parents' campsite to cook the rattlesnake while Tana and Margaret headed for Oogay's camp. Back at the lean-to Margaret watched Tana paint designs on the backs of her hands and in the outside corners of her eyes, using a wet lump of red clay for paint and a passenger pigeon tail feather as a brush. Tana looked at Margaret and said, "I cannot reach the tattoo on my back. Please color it in for me." She handed Margaret the feather paintbrush.

Margaret rubbed the tip of the feather on the lump of red clay and brushed the color inside the outline of Tana's mammoth tattoo. While Margaret worked she asked Tana questions.

"When do women of the Mammoth Clan get their tattoos?"

"It depends," Tana replied. "Some wait until they are married or have a baby. Some are tattooed when a loved one dies."

"When did you get your tattoo?" Margaret finished coloring Tana's tattoo and gave the feather brush back to Tana.

"I was young, maybe a year older than Mutt is now. Rom was just a baby. My grandmother, whom I loved very much, came to live with my da and Gam and me and Rom. One clear winter night, when everyone else was asleep, I wandered out of our hut to look at the stars. I became lost and could not find my way home. Lucky for me, Gam woke up to nurse Rom and noticed I was missing."

"Gam had to stay with Rom, so just my da and my grandmother ran out into the darkness to look for me. My grandmother found me shivering under a birch tree. She called for my da and he carried me back to the hut. Once I warmed up I was OK, but my grandmother had caught a chill and soon became sick with the cough that never stops. When she died four days later I was sitting next to her, and her hand was on my back. Afterward I decided to have a mammoth tattoo put on that spot."

Tana told the story of her tattoo in a matter-of-fact way, but when she finished her eyes were moist.

Margaret pondered Tana's story while she helped Tana put away the red clay makeup. Then Margaret began to tell Tana a story.

"I love my grandmother very much. I've called her Nana since I could talk. When I was little, Nana and I played a game called 'lump.' I'd hide under the covers and when Nana entered my room to tuck me in she'd say, 'Goodness, where's Margaret?' Then she'd say, 'And what's this lump under the covers?' She would tickle me through the covers and I would laugh and laugh. When I finally ran out of breath, I would stick my arm out from the covers and she would gently grab me, which meant the game was over."

"That sounds like a wonderful game," said Tana.

"Tana?"

"Yes?"

"May I get a mammoth tattoo on my arm?"

* * * * *

Margaret did not turn away as the woman from the Caribou Clan prepared to give Margaret her mammoth tattoo. The woman's tools were simple. The needle was a splinter of caribou bone, shaped more or less like a very sharp nail. A groove had been carved from the wide head of the needle down to the sharp point.

The tattoo artist had coiled a piece of yarn around the wide head of the needle. She held the needle in her right hand and a small amount of ink in her cupped left hand. The ink was made from charcoal dust mixed with water. The artist dipped the fat end of the needle into the ink and the yarn soaked up the black liquid. She then held the needle like a pencil with the point touching the skin of Margaret's right forearm. Ink ran down the groove in the bone and a tiny bead formed at the sharp point. The woman began to poke up and down, very fast.

The poking felt like a bee sting and Margaret had to bite her lip to keep from crying out. After five to ten pokes the ink was forced under the skin, leaving a permanent black dot.

The poking stopped and the artist applied more ink to the yarn-end of the needle. Tana, who was sitting on the ground behind Margaret and holding her around the waist, asked, "Do you want to stop?"

Margaret shook her head, "No."

The poking began again and another dot appeared next to the first. The process was repeated many times and a line of ink dots slowly appeared beneath the skin. Margaret's eyes filled with tears and some ran down her cheeks, but she did not move.

After an hour Margaret was not sure she could go on. She decided to cry "Stop!" but before the words came out the artist said, "All done."

There was a little blood on top of the skin. Tana dabbed it away with a handful of dry grass. On Margaret's forearm, as clear as day but no bigger than the surface of a quarter, was a tiny mammoth tattoo.

"You were very brave," Tana whispered in Margaret's ear. They stood up and Margaret held her arm tattoo next to the tattoo on Tana's back. Tana's tattoo was bigger, but otherwise they were an exact match.

CHAPTER 13
DANCE

The heavens were clear and the moon was almost full. More stars than a person could count shone against the black of the night sky. There was no wind so the sparks from the three roaring bonfires shot straight up. The people of the four clans were sitting in a wide arc in front of the fires.

Oogay's family sat with the other families of the Mammoth Clan. Margaret, Tur, and Mutt sat cross-legged in the front. Oogay, Tana, and Gam sat directly behind them. Rom and Podi were sitting with the Lion Clan. Everyone was eating bison that had been roasted earlier by men of the Caribou Clan, and pancakes that had been prepared by the women of the Beaver Clan. The pancakes were made from a wild grain called "manoo," and cooked on hot flat stones.

Margaret tried three times to count the people sitting in front of the fires, but she always lost track after her count passed three hundred. In frustration she turned to Tur and asked, "How many people do you think are here tonight?"

Tur turned his head to the left and right. He replied, "All of them."

Boys placed new wood on each fire. When the boys were done, eight men stood up and moved toward the center fire. Three men carried single sided drums made from caribou hide stretched over a frame of sticks, and a small club carved from a knot of wood. Two others carried shakers made from a tube of deerskin filled with pebbles. The last three carried trumpets made from hollowed mastodon tusks. The men stood together and began to play.

The drums and rattles gave the beat while the trumpeters blew slow deep notes. When the band finished, an old man wearing the red crest feathers of a log cock in his grey hair and holding a staff of polished ironwood in his right hand, walked to the center of the space between the fires and the people and began to speak.

"I thank our brothers of the Caribou Clan for the bison supper, and our sisters of the Beaver Clan for their delicious manoo bread. Many a man has married a Beaver woman just so he can taste manoo bread more than once a year." The crowd laughed at his joke.

"Before the dancing begins we will have a wrestling contest between the four clans.I will draw a circle here in the dirt. If a contestant throws his opponent out of the circle, he wins the match. I will be the judge. Who wants to go first?"

"I, Chuz, will wrestle for the Caribou Clan," said a short, well-muscled young man about Rom's age.

Bo was quick to stand up. "I am Bo of the Beaver Clan. I will wrestle Chuz."

Oogay whispered to Tana, "The youngster from the Beaver Clan towers above the young man from the Caribou Clan. This will not be a fair fight."

The judge drew a large circle on the ground. Chuz and Bo faced each other, crouching. One of the drummers beat his drum three times, and on the third beat the wrestlers ran toward each other.

Chuz was able to duck and grab the taller Bo around the waist. At first it looked like the shorter man had the advantage. But Bo was able to stretch a long leg behind Chuz and trip him. As Chuz struggled to stand up, Bo grabbed his left foot with both hands and began to spin around. Chuz was forced to hop along on one leg while flailing at the air with both hands. Bo gave a great heave and Chuz went flying out of the circle and onto his backside.

The judge raised Bo's right arm and shouted, "The winner!" Bo, breathing heavily, waived to the cheering Beaver Clan.

During the first match Rom and Podi had walked around the ring of spectators to stand with Oogay and Tana. Rom leaned over to Tur and quietly asked, "Why is Bo wearing your lion necklace?"

"It's a long story," Tur mumbled.

"So tell me."

Mutt interrupted. "That Bo fellow made Tur give him the necklace. Otherwise, he was going to cook my puppy!"

"Is that true?" Rom asked. Tur looked at the ground and said nothing.

"It's true!" Margaret exclaimed. "And Bo called you a liar."

Rom turned and stared at Bo. Bo was about to wrestle again, this time with a teenager from the Lion Clan. The drum was struck three times and the young men rushed together. The wrestler from the Lion Clam was almost as tall as Bo so the match lasted several minutes, with both contestants shoving and grunting and trying to gain the upper hand. The man from the Lion Clan found traction and began to push Bo toward the edge of the circle. Suddenly Bo threw a low blow and punched the other man in the loincloth. The man groaned and stumbled forward, out of the circle. As the Lion Clan's man went down, Bo kicked him in the behind for good measure.

"That's fighting dirty," Oogay said to Rom. It was plain to see that Bo had won with a dishonorable punch, so this time the cheering was subdued.

A little boy carried a hollow gourd filled with water out to Bo. He took a gulp and poured the rest over his head.

"Is there anyone else who dares to try his luck?" Bo crowed.

"Me."

Bo turned to see Rom walking into the ring.

"You!" Bo spat. "I warn you, Mammoth man, that I'm more dangerous than the lion you claim you killed. Come here if you dare, and I'll show Podi she has chosen a weakling."

Bo jumped up and down on his toes and then went into a crouch. Rom bent down and slapped the ground with the palms of his hands. They circled each other, looking for an advantage.

Bo lunged first and almost caught Rom between the legs with one long arm. Rom kicked his legs out straight and collapsed on top of the bigger man. Bo's chin slammed into the dirt and he saw stars.

Before Bo could recover, Rom locked his arms behind Bo's neck and dragged the taller man to the edge of the circle. With a push to the back of the head, Rom sent Bo stumbling out of the ring. Bo fell into a pile, groaning. Rom reached down and tore the lion tooth necklace from Bo's neck. Rom did not wait to be declared the winner. He walked back to Tur and handed him the necklace, saying, "This belongs to you."

* * * * *

The musicians gathered again and began to play. This time the beat was faster and the notes higher. A line of dancers, all women and girls from the Caribou Clan, hopped and skipped in unison until they were in the middle of the space between the fires and the audience. They were wearing their finest dresses and no moccasins. Many had adorned their feet and hands and faces with red and blue paint. The pace of the music quickened and the dancers moved faster, hopping and twirling in unison. They held their arms in the air to symbolize antlers. The men of the Caribou Clan whooped and whistled and cheered their women on.

"They're very good," Margaret said to Tur.

"Yes," he replied, "but wait until you see Ma dance. Nobody dances better than she does!"

Margaret looked over where Tana had been standing but she and Gam had disappeared. Oogay was holding the baby. He smiled at Margaret and motioned for her to join him. She stood up and went to stand by his side.

Next came dancers from the Lion Clan. Several had bits of lion fur sewn into their dresses. They also wore paint, orange like the color of smilodon fur. They dug the dirt with their feet and clawed the air with their hands. Podi had rejoined her family and was dancing next to her mother.

Soon the women of the Beaver Clan took the stage. They made paddling motions like a swimming beaver as they moved back and forth before the audience.

Finally it was time for the dance of the Mammoth women. "You may join the dancers if you like," Oogay said to Margaret.

She looked up at him and said, "I don't know how."

"You wear the tattoo of the clan. You are one of us. Just do what the other young girls do and you'll be fine."

Margaret left Oogay and ran over to stand in a line that was forming at the edge of the dance area. The dancers of the Mammoth Clan had arranged their clothing so that their mammoth tattoos were plain to see. Margaret stood on her tip toes to learn who would lead them out to dance. It was Gam.

The music slowed a bit as the mammoth women filed out to dance. The girls in front of Margaret slowly stomped their feet as they walked, and held out one arm to sway back and forth like a trunk. Margaret copied them.

The dancers made a slow circle, stopped and separated into two groups. Each group stood in place stomping and clapping with the beat of the drums. Two men appeared from behind the fires, each painted from head to toe in black soot and carrying a bright white mammoth tusk. The men stood perfectly still with the tusks arcing skyward to form the outline of a door. The crowd began to stomp and clap in unison with the dancers. Then *she* appeared.

A solo dancer, clothed in a bright white buckskin dress, her face boldly painted in streaks of white and pink, ran out from behind the fires and jumped to a stop under the mammoth tusks. She threw her arms up in the air and shouted "Tee-Kai-Koa," which was an ancient word for mammoth. The crowd roared and stood up as one. The dancer in the white dress began to whirl and kick like a person gone mad.

The dancer in the white dress began to whirl and kick like a person gone mad.

The other mammoth women moved in to join her as the drums beat ever louder and faster. The horns began to blast and the crowd responded by singing and dancing in place. All of the dancers were yelling or chanting at the top of their lungs. The soot covered men laid down their mammoth tusks and put the dancer in the white dress on their shoulders. From her high perch she swayed back and forth while others approached to touch her hands or her feet. The noise of the crowd was deafening and Margaret felt like she might be trampled. She was shoved from behind until she was within touching distance of the crazy woman in the white dress. The dancer made brief eye contact with Margaret and smiled. It was Tana! Then she was carried away by the men in black.

* * * * *

The next day the Oogay family, like everyone else at the Gathering, was slow to wake up. Margaret was the first to arise. She put on her moccasins and walked away from the camp in order to go to the bathroom in private.

Margaret pushed through a line of young spruce and found herself at the edge of a broad meadow. Scattered across the opening were two dozen wild horses led by a single stallion. They were the color of chocolate milk, with their manes and tails darker than their bodies. Colts were scattered among the mares. The colts were the same color as the adults, but had dark stripes on their rear ends.

"There were many more horses when I was a child." Gam stood next to Margaret and coughed.

"Where did the other horses go?" Margaret asked.

"Nobody knows, child. Every spring the herds just seem to be smaller than the year before."

"Do the people of the clans ever ride them?"

"Ride a horse? Why would somebody want to do that? It sounds like a good way to get kicked or bitten. But I like horses, especially if they're cooked real slow."

The trees on the other side of the meadow began to shake and a very large bear ambled into the clearing. The horses watched nervously as the bear stood on his hind legs and sniffed the air.

He looks like the grizzly bears on television, thought Margaret, *except his nose is flat and short.*

"That's an old bear," Gam whispered, "and too slow to catch a horse. But he could still run down you or me. Let's head back to camp."

On the walk back to camp Gam's breathing became raspy and she had to stop twice to cough. The ground was red where she spat.

"Gam, are you alright?" Margaret asked worriedly.

"I'm fine, child. Last night's dancing wore me out. I'll be better as the day warms up. Besides, tomorrow you and I have something very important to do."

"What's that?"

"We're starting on a journey to the mammoth graveyard to collect bones and tusks. Soon the Gathering will come to an end and we need ivory to trade with the other clans before everybody goes their separate ways."

"Will the whole family go with us?"

"No, it's better for the baby and Mutt to stay behind because graveyard spirits like to steal the very young. And Tana needs to stay to arrange Rom and Podi's marriage contract with Podi's mother. Oogay is going to lead one more hunt. So, it will be you and me and Tur and Rom and Podi making the trip to the graveyard. We can be there in two days. As we walk north there will be fewer trees and the ground will get colder."

"Then I'd better sew some new leather to the bottom of my moccasins."

PART III
THE BIG ICE

CHAPTER 14
PECCARY PIGS

The family arose extra early the next morning. Breakfast was strips of smoked bison and dried grapes. Tana supervised the unpacking of the winter clothes before she left with Mutt and the baby to visit with Podi's ma. The puppy followed Mutt. The big dogs stayed with Rom.

Oogay was preparing to go hunting with men from the Caribou Clan. The boy who had been gored by the bison was dead. The bison had to be tracked and killed so the boy's spirit could rest in peace. Before leaving, Oogay pulled Tur aside for a private talk.

"Gam says the mark by your eye means someday you'll be an important person. Maybe she's right, I don't know. . ." Oogay started to say more, but his voice trailed off. He dug through his shoulder bag and produced a beautiful chert dagger. The blade was fixed to a piece of caribou horn, and the horn had been polished to a bright shine.

"I made this for you. It's not a child's toy but the knife of a man. On your journey Rom must protect Podi and you must protect Margaret, and you both must protect Gam. Do you understand?"

Tur thought to himself, *I'm not sure Podi or Margaret need protecting, and only a fool would pick a fight with Gam!* But Oogay was staring at him, so Tur answered "Yes, Da."

"Good boy. I'll see you again in several days. Mind Rom and Gam, watch the sky for bad weather, and listen for voices in the wind."

* * * * *

It had been two months since Margaret had seen her pajamas. Gam held them out to her and said, "Put these on under your dress. When we get close to the Big Ice the wind will be much colder."

Next Gam produced deerskin leggings for everyone. They were like leather socks that stretched from the top of your moccasin to above your knee. The leggings were lined with downy feathers collected from passenger pigeons. The down made the leggings very warm and soft.

Rom tied a bundle to each of the dogs with a harness made from strips of leather. Frik hauled a bison robe, dry kindling, and extra skins to repair moccasins. Frak was burdened with spears, an axe for chopping ivory, and spare wedges of chert. Gam, Rom, Podi, Tur, and Margaret each carried a shoulder bag stuffed with personal items, gooey balls of caribou fat and ground beechnuts wrapped in strips of bison, and paw paws. Tur carried his new dagger in a thick leather sleeve that Podi had stitched to the back of his shirt.

They followed a well-worn trail out of camp, always with the morning sun on their right shoulder. By midday the trail became overgrown. The group stopped to eat lunch and rest while Rom grabbed the axe and continued ahead. He returned a half hour later, sweating and breathing hard. "I marked a trail. Follow it while I go ahead again." He stood up and disappeared the way he had come.

So it went for the rest of the afternoon. Gam, Podi, Margaret, and Tur plodded along, followed by the dogs. Every hour or so they would catch up to Rom. They usually found him sitting on a log or stump, carefully removing thorns and brambles from his moccasins and leggings. Gam and Rom would talk between themselves for a bit, after which Rom would disappear again into the woods.

As the day wore on the trees along the trail got shorter while the grass got taller. Now and then a wet wind would blow into Margaret's face. Sometimes it would sting. When she wiped her face with her hand, she could feel tiny bits of melting ice.

Rounding the top of a hill, Tur, Margaret, Podi, and Gam almost tripped over Rom. He was crouched low to the ground.

Rom put a finger to his lips. "Shhhh, be still." Frik and Frak began to whine. "Quiet!" whispered Rom at the dogs as he untied their bundles. They followed him into the long grass. Tur said nothing as he picked up two throwing spears and followed his uncle.

"Where are Rom and Tur going?" Margaret whispered to Podi.

"To catch supper, I think."

Gam was looking at something on the ground. She poked it with a twig and smelled the end. "I thought so. Pig for supper!"

Before Gam could say more, the grass parted and a pack of snarling, grunting pigs burst by the girls. The pigs had flat heads, bristling black fur, sharp feet, and curled tusks on their snouts. One of the smaller pigs ran headlong into Margaret and knocked her down. On the heels of the pigs came Frik and Frak, sprinting and howling. Frak caught a big sow by the rear leg but let go when the sow kicked him hard under the chin. Close behind the dogs came Rom and Tur, high stepping over clumps of trampled grass. They came to a stop by the girls, hands on hips and breathing hard. Rom had a nasty gash on his left forearm.

"Did you see 'em, did you see 'em, Gam?" croaked Tur.

"Yes, boy, we saw them."

"They were hard to miss," said Margaret, as she stood up and began picking dirt, grass, and pig bristles out of her braids.

"Rom, you're bleeding!" Podi ran to him and gently took hold of his arm. Rom was embarrassed at Podi's fussing, but he stood still and let Podi bind the cut with a knot of long grass stems.

Tur, having caught his breath, continued his story. "You should have seen Rom! He snuck up on the boar and jabbed him with a spear. It was the biggest pig ever!" Tur stretched his arms as wide as they would go.

"I've seen bigger," said Rom. He grunted as Podi tightened his arm bandage.

"That old boar, he turned right around and charged Rom. The spear came loose and broke in two. The pig tried to bite Rom."

"That's when he got my arm with a tusk," Rom interrupted. "The dogs came charging in and the boar turned around again and headed toward all of you. The smaller pigs went with him."

"They found us," said Margaret.

At that moment Frik and Frak returned, tails wagging. The pigs had escaped but the dogs looked proud of themselves anyway.

* * * * *

As the sun began to set on their left, the five travelers stopped for the night. Podi and Margaret gathered wood and started a fire. Rom and Tur built a lean-to under a lone white pine, using the soft fallen needles for a floor and the bison robe for a blanket. Free of their bundles, Frik and Frak ran baying into the bushes. Half an hour later they returned, each dog with one end of a dead armadillo clamped in its teeth. They proceeded to eat the scaly beast, all the time growling at each other.

Everyone squatted around the camp fire. Food was shared. Gam did not say very much. She just stared into the flames, her bony arms wrapped tightly around her knobby knees. She looked worn out.

"Gam," said Margaret, "let's sit close so it will be easier to trade stories." She cuddled Gam in her arms and was surprised to find that the old woman was shivering.

"Thank you, little daughter," whispered Gam. She closed her eyes and leaned against Margaret with a sigh.

Rom and Tur had never seen Gam so frail. It made them worry, but being men they had to pretend everything was fine and say nothing.

"When I was little" – it was Podi who broke the silence – "my ma told me about going to the mammoth graveyard with Gam and Tana. My ma was no older than you" – Podi nodded at Margaret – "when she made the trip, and Tana was younger than Mutt. Ma said the Big Ice was closer to the graveyard back then, and herds of mammoth roamed over the open ground, eating the thick grass. Their manure was piled everywhere, attracting grouse and prairie voles hungry for a snack."

"Yuck," said Tur.

Podi smiled and continued. "Ma said she soon learned not to step where the grass was greenest, unless she wanted to lose her moccasin in a squishy pile of poo!" Everyone laughed, which made Gam open her eyes.

Gam coughed and said, "You children are a noisy bunch. Let's get some sleep because tomorrow is another long walk." Rom and Podi had to help Gam stand up, and she fell asleep as soon as they tucked her under one edge of the bison robe. Margaret and Tur slept on their backs under the middle of the robe, while Rom and Podi cuddled on the other edge. Frik and Frak lay at the feet of everyone, staring into the darkness. The dogs knew they were being watched from beyond the dying fire.

CHAPTER 15
GRAVEYARD

Margaret wanted to be the first to catch sight of the mammoth graveyard, so she and Tur strode ahead of the others. Margaret was nervously braiding stalks of grass into green twine as she went. Tur followed behind, walking backwards while practicing birdcalls.

"WHEE-ah, chuck-chuck," crowed Tur.

"Blue Jay," said Margaret. She did not turn around but kept walking.

"Kip-kip-kip, ZEEE."

"Grass Sparrow."

"You're getting pretty good," Tur admitted. "How about this one? O-ka-lee."

Margaret did not answer.

Tur tried again. "O-ka-lee."

Still no answer.

"It's a red-winged blackbird; you know –" Tur did not finish because he backed into Margaret, who had stopped in her tracks.

"Tur, quit fooling around and look!" Tur did as she asked.

The high grass was gone. In its place was a wide open meadow where every blade of grass had been grazed to a nubbin. A few lone trees stood here and there, stripped of all but their highest branches. Some of the trees looked like they had been pushed over by a giant hand. Far to the north was the outline of a tall ridge.

There were bones everywhere. Piles of bones. BIG bones. And skulls. Jawbones filled with wide flat teeth. And curved ivory tusks that were longer than a man was tall. In the middle of the field was a large lodge made completely of skulls, thigh bones, and tusks.

Tur gave a low whistle.

"You think that's the Graveyard?" Margaret whispered.

"Of course it is," Gam answered. She and Podi and Rom had caught up to Margaret and Tur. Gam had to lean on Rom as she walked. She sat down to catch her breath.

"When a mammoth is very old, it comes here. It lies down with eyes closed. Members of its family stand guard, stroking the old one's face and forehead with their trunks. It is a quiet death. In a few weeks only the bones remain. Sometimes, months or even years later, the mammoth's family will return to stack the bones in a pile."

"Did the mammoths build the lodge?" Margaret asked.

"No child, it was built by members of our clan. Long ago the spirits of the mammoths gave us permission to collect their tusks. In thanks, our people built the lodge so those spirits have a safe place to sleep at night. Before we leave, we will fix any part of the lodge that needs repair." With Podi for support on one side and Margaret on the other, Gam slowly stood up. Everyone walked together to the entrance of the lodge.

Frik and Frak trotted up to the door and sniffed, but would not go inside. They whined and backed away.

"Well, at least tonight we'll have a dry place to sleep, out of this nasty weather," said Rom. A cold wind had arrived from the north, and the clouds overhead were getting darker by the minute.

"I'm afraid you and Tur and the dogs must sleep outside," said Podi. "My ma told me only women may sleep in the lodge." She gave Rom a sympathetic kiss on the cheek.

"Is that true, Gam?" asked Tur. He did not relish the idea of sleeping outside during a thunderstorm.

"Off you go," Gam told the disappointed Tur. "Break up one of the dead trees for firewood, and another for a lean-to. Podi and Margaret will burn a small fire inside the lodge, and you and Rom and the dogs can keep a big fire going outside. The lodge will act as a windbreak from the north wind." With that, Gam and the girls ducked inside the lodge.

* * * * *

By the time darkness fell, Rom and Tur had built their lean-to against the south side of the lodge and had built a roaring fire. The black clouds decided to drop snow instead of rain. The snow melted when it hit the warm ground. Soon there was thick fog everywhere.

Rom and Tur sat with their backs against the outside wall of the lodge, dozing. The big bones of the wall, heated by the little inside fire, felt warm against their backs. Frik and Frak lay at their feet.

The wind began to die down and it stopped snowing. Moonbeams began to shine through breaks in the clouds. That's when the howling started.

It was the wolf song, beginning as a throaty growl and rising to a high pitched "Oooooooh-a-wooooooo!" The first wolf was quickly joined by a second, then a third and a fourth. Rom and Tur awoke and reached for their spears. Tur looked anxiously at his uncle.

"It's the big male with the white face and his pack," said Rom in a low voice. "They must have followed us from the Gathering."

"Do they want to eat us?" whispered Tur.

"A wolf will eat anything, but that big male is a clever fellow. I think he's hoping we will lead him to bigger prey."

The howls became louder and longer, as if the wolves were inviting the moon to drop from the sky and join them. Frik and Frak stood up, legs set apart, heads down. The fur on their backs and around their throats was bristly. They started to growl.

"Easy!" commanded Rom. "Stay."

Frik turned his large head and looked at Rom as if to say, "I know you want us to remain by the fire, but our family is in danger." The big dog turned and sprinted into the dark fog. Frak galloped after him.

"No!" cried Tur, and he jumped up to run after the dogs. Rom tripped him with the end of his spear pole.

"They're gone. There's nothing we can do until morning. Sit down and don't wake the women."

A little while later the howling stopped.

* * * * *

Rom did not know that Margaret and Podi were awake. The girls had heard the wolves, but their attention was on Gam. Even with the girls on each side of her and the bison robe pulled over all three, Gam was shivering. It became hard for her to breathe. Podi pulled Gam's head and shoulders into her lap while Margaret gently rubbed the old woman's forehead and cheek. Gam smiled and closed her eyes. After a few minutes she quit shivering. Then she was gone.

CHAPTER 16
FUNERAL

I have never been so miserable, thought Margaret. She leaned against Podi in the cold morning fog, the bison robe pulled tightly around them. The girls watched as Rom and Tur lashed together a funeral cot under a tall dead spruce tree. The cot was as high off the ground as Rom was tall. The legs were made from mammoth tusks and the bed was made from parts of the leather dog harnesses.

The dog harnesses were used to build the cot because Frik and Frak were dead. When it became light enough to follow tracks in the wet ground, Rom and Tur had gone to find the dogs. They found Frak at the edge of the high grass. He lifeless body was bitten in many places, and one of his front legs was broken. He had bravely tried to make it back to camp.

Deeper into the tall weeds, next to a rocky outcrop, they found Frik's body. He too had suffered many bites. Next to Frik was a dead wolf, a yearling male.

Rom kneeled next to Frik and wrapped his arms around the big dog's head. Rom rocked back and forth, tears streaming silently down his cheeks. It was the first time Tur had seen Rom cry. They buried the dogs side by side, under a pile of stones, and returned to the Graveyard to build Gam's funeral cot.

Podi removed a clam shell filled with caribou fat from her shoulder bag. She mixed in some charcoal to make black paste. In silence Podi painted a wide stripe on Margaret's face that stretched from one ear, across the eyes and nose to the other ear. Margaret did the same for Podi. Then Podi painted the left side of Rom's face with the paste, while Margaret used a small bit of the sticky stuff to paint a star over the birthmark behind Tur's right eye.

The girls spread the bison robe on the ground and went inside the lodge for Gam's body. With Rom and Tur's help the old woman was laid in the middle of the robe. Rom placed a polished spear point on Gam's left side. The girls removed small shells from their braids and placed them on Gam's right. Tur took the smilodon tooth necklace from around his neck and put it on his dead grandmother's hands. The girls closed the edges of the robe like a snug blanket. The head and feet were wrapped with the remaining pieces of the dog harnesses. Quietly they lifted Gam's cloaked body up onto the bed of the cot.

After a few minutes of silence Podi asked, "What do we do now?"

"We can't return the way we came," answered Rom. "The wolves are waiting for us out in the tall grass. We need to keep walking north, toward the Big Ice. Maybe the wolves will tire of the chase and go away."

* * * * *

They had walked for about an hour when the fog disappeared. What had seemed like a far off hill was really a sheet of dirty ice that stretched from east to west as far as the eye could see. A cold wind blew off the ice and into their faces.

The four wanderers stopped at midday for a meal and a warming fire. They lined their moccasins with new handfuls of dry grass. *I would give everything I own for a pair of wool socks,* thought Margaret.

Podi sat next to Rom, his arms around her shoulders. She looked very tired. His left arm was red and swollen where it had been stabbed by the boar's tusk. They leaned against each other and closed their eyes.

By comparison, Tur was all business. The few trees that dotted the prairie were not tall enough to make a good watchtower. After staring ahead with hands on his hips for a few minutes, Tur grabbed Margaret's hand and said, "Come with me."

They jogged north until Margaret's side began to ache. "Tur, I have to stop. Please!"

Tur was embarrassed that he had run his friend ragged. "I'm sorry Margaret, of course we can stop. I think we've gone far enough anyway."

They sat so Margaret could catch her breath. After a few minutes Tur stood up and walked over to a short spruce that was only a foot taller than he. "Please come here and climb up on my shoulders, Margaret."

Using the small tree to steady herself, Margaret did as he asked. She put one foot on each side of Tur's neck. He firmly held one of her ankles in each of his hands. The top of the spruce was just below her waist, so it was easy to hang on for balance.

"What do you see?" he asked.

Margaret looked back over her shoulder at the way they'd come. "I see Rom and Podi. They're slowly walking this way, following our footprints."

She twisted slowly to her right and then to her left. "The Big Ice seems to go in both directions forever. There is a river at the bottom of the ice wall. And, and . . ."

"And what?"

"Tur, I think we've found the mammoths!"

CHAPTER 17
MAMMOTH

They set up camp along the south bank of the river. The Big Ice began its rise about a half mile north of the river. The edge of the ice was melting into countless trickles of water. Most of the runoff ended up in the river. Pieces of grass and sticks and dirt that fell into the river were quickly carried off to the west by the current.

In some places the river was frozen over. Margaret remembered how Joe had warned her to stay off river ice in the winter. "It might look solid," he would say, "but the current causes weak spots. Stay off the ice like your life depends on it!"

A hundred paces from the camp grazed the most magnificent animals that Margaret had ever seen. It was a family of Columbian mammoths. There were three cows, the youngest of which had a male calf following her around. The oldest cow, the baby's grandmother, kept an eye on the four humans while the others calmly ate the thick grass along the riverbank. The baby pulled at the grass with his trunk and sometimes put it in his mouth, but he always spit it out.

Standing quite far away was a bull. The bull was a giant. He was almost twice as tall as Old Doc and three times as tall as a man. The cows were taller than a modern elephant, but much shorter than the bull. Each of the bull's legs was a big around as a tree trunk. All four of the adults had large domed heads and fat trunks that extended to the ground. White tusks curved down and away from their mouths. The bull's tusks were so long that Rom could have stretched out on one with room to spare.

The cows and the bull were covered with tough brown hide. Long strands of black hair grew down from the middle of their backs, but the hair was not thick enough to hide the skin underneath. The baby looked like the adults in some ways, but was different in others. His trunk did not yet reach the ground, his tusks barely showed, his belly was plump and his legs were short, and the top of his head had not yet developed a bump. Also, the long hairs down the middle of his back were blonde.

"Margaret, the baby mammoth has yellow hair just like you," teased Tur. At that moment the baby pooped a squirty mess.

"Well, there's things about him that remind me of you, too," Margaret replied. She held her nose and laughed.

Margaret's laughter caught the baby's attention. He trotted toward her. *For having such big flat feet, he's pretty quick*, she thought. Standing as still as possible, Margaret slowly removed a paw paw from her shoulder bag and held it out toward the baby. The little mammoth stopped and looked Margaret up and down with his big round eyes. He stuck out his baby-sized trunk and breathed in the smell of the very ripe paw paw. The smell made him bat his long eyelashes.

The baby snuffed and came closer.

"That's it," said Margaret softly. "I won't hurt you. Go ahead, this is for you." She stretched out her arm as far as it would go with the paw paw at the very end of her fingers. The baby snatched the fruit and for an instant the end of his trunk touched Margaret's hand. It was warm and soft as velvet.

The baby's mother had been watching. Something as small and toothless as a human probably couldn't hurt her calf. After all, the baby was roughly the size of a washer and dryer placed side by side. Still, a mother can't be too careful! The cow trumpeted a high pitched "toot" and the baby immediately ran back to his mother's side. He dropped the paw paw and stuck his head up under the cow's front leg to nurse.

"I guess he prefers his ma's milk to an over ripe paw paw," joked Tur.

"I suppose," replied Margaret. She was secretly thrilled that the baby had been willing to take food right out of her hand.

While Margaret was tempting the baby mammoth with a paw paw, upstream the bull had found a tree trunk stuck in the river bank. He wrapped his great trunk around the log and lifted it clear out of the water. The bull waived the timber like a huge baseball bat, and then began to scratch his back with it. The bull's antics attracted the baby's attention. The calf trotted toward the big bull and stopped just short of the big male's left tusk. The bull stared down at the calf and kept scratching.

The baby turned toward the riverbank and began rooting through the brush with his little trunk. He pulled up a white sumac sapling and triumphantly carried it over to show the bull. The calf began to scratch himself with the sapling. That seemed to make the baby more interesting to the bull, because he dropped his tree trunk and extended his long trunk toward the baby. The calf looked up at his father and made a small bleat.

What came next happened in the blink of an eye. The calf's mother ran up and rammed her forehead into the left hindquarter of the bull. He was knocked off balance but did not fall down. The bull steadied himself, threw his head back and bellowed, "Raw-loooo." He snorted and stamped the ground.

While the bull was making his big fuss, the mother mammoth herded her baby back to the other cows. They stood together facing the bull, with the baby hiding behind.

The bull began to calm down. He stared at the three cows for a few minutes, shook his giant tusks from side to side once, then turned and walked away upstream. His antics had been watched in fascination by the four humans.

"I guess Ma and Da are no longer in love," quipped Rom.

"You're wrong," replied Podi. "Da just needs to learn who's in charge of the children!"

"I think the father likes the baby," Margaret offered, "but maybe the mother thinks the father plays too rough?"

"Who cares?" said Tur, "they're just beasts. Who wants to help me catch some fish for dinner?"

* * * * *

As the sun set the river came alive with hungry grayling. Dozens of the shiny green fish took turns biting at the flies and gnats that unwisely landed on the surface. Each time a grayling rose to eat a bug, Margaret caught a glimpse of its head, black dots behind the gills and a long glittering top fin.

Podi and Margaret got busy braiding grass stems to make fishing line. Tur pulled some small dried bones from his shoulder bag and tied them to the ends of the lines as hooks. For bait they caught some grasshoppers in the tall grass.

Margaret and Tur did the fishing while Rom and Podi stood guard. The mammoth family had walked downstream and the bull seemed to have wandered away. Still, Rom thought it best to keep an eye out for trouble.

It's not easy to hook a grayling with a bone hook. The trick is to jerk the line at just the right time and hope the fish will fly out of the water far enough to fall onto the bank, instead of back in the river.

Tur and Margaret both had nibbles but the wriggling grayling kept getting off the hook. Finally, with a long pull of her wrist, Margaret yanked a flopping fish onto dry land. She quickly baited her hook and caught another.

"How are you doing that?" demanded Tur. He did not like being bested by a girl at fishing, or at anything else for that matter.

"My dad calls it 'snagging.' The trick is to give a long yank and not let the line go slack. Like this." Margaret went through the motion and another grayling was on the shore.

Tur tried to copy Margaret, but his next fish fell off the hook just short of the bank. "Stupid, stupid, stupid!" he cursed.

"One more thing," said Margaret. "You gotta hold your tongue just right."

"My tongue?"

"Yup. Like this." She rolled her tongue and stuck it out between her lips.

Tur looked skeptical but gave it a try. With his tongue poking from the corner of his mouth, he flicked a grasshopper out onto the water. A grayling rose and took the bait. Tur yanked back as Margaret had showed him, and the beautiful fish ended up at his feet.

"Mar-get, thit wukked." He pulled his tongue back in and repeated, "It worked!"

Margaret laughed so hard she started to slide down the riverbank. Tur threw down his line and caught her. Their noses touched. Suddenly Margaret kissed Tur square on the mouth, like she had seen Podi kiss Rom. The kiss startled Tur and he almost dropped her. Margaret twisted loose from his arms, picked up two handfuls of fish, and skipped to Podi singing, "Look what I caught for dinner."

Tur watched her go and wondered, *What was that all about?* But he sort of liked it.

* * * * *

By nightfall the mammoth family had moved farther downstream, too far away to be seen or heard by the humans. Podi, Rom, Margaret, and Tur built a small lean-to, using the bison robe as a common blanket. Rom and Podi lay on their sides with their backs to Tur and Margaret. Feeling ignored, Tur and Margaret lay on their backs and gazed up at the night sky. It was cloudy, but now and then a star would shine through the gloom.

"What do you think stars are made of?" Tur asked Margaret.

"My dad says they're big balls of hot air."

"What?" Tur snorted. "That's the craziest thing I've ever heard! I think stars are spirits, and they twinkle when they talk to each other."

"My dad also says that some stars are not stars at all, but pieces of rock and ice. Sometimes they crash to the ground and make a mess. That's how I ended up in the river the day you and I met."

"Margaret, you tell good stories." Tur yawned. A moment later he was snoring.

Margaret continued to look up. The clouds thinned and the stars burst into view. *Lots of shooting stars tonight*, Margaret noticed. She decided to count every one as they zipped across the blackness, but before she got to a hundred she was fast asleep.

CHAPTER 18
BRIDGE

The four travelers had just lit their morning fire when the flaming meteor came roaring into view from the south. It streaked directly overhead and disappeared into the distant clouds above the Big Ice. A great boom filled the sky, louder than thunder. The noise made hundreds of black scoters and other river ducks take flight in terror.

Rom and Podi and Tur were also terrified. They dove inside the lean-to and covered their heads with the bison robe. Rom clutched his biggest spear.

Margaret stayed outside, watching the sky fill with birds. "Come back to the fire," she called to her friends. "The meteor's gone and won't be back."

Podi was first to crawl out from beneath the robe. "Margaret, how do you know about such things?"

"I've seen one before."

"Well, I haven't," said Rom as he stood up, "and I don't want to see another! Today we turn south and begin walking back to the Gathering. With luck the wolves have moved on."

"I think our luck has run out," replied Tur. He pointed upstream. Sitting on their haunches, staring at the humans, were three dire wolves, a yearling and two adults. The biggest had a white blaze across his face.

* * * * *

The mammoth cows were too far downstream to see the wolves, but they could smell them. The grandmother snuffed and snorted and waved her great head from side to side. The other cows did likewise. They began to trot along the riverbank, away from the wolves, with the baby mammoth doing his best to keep up.

The little herd reached a place where three tree trunks had become stuck on some rocks at the bottom of the river. The current had pushed smaller branches and sticks up against the trunks, which made a rickety bridge from one bank of the river to the other. Smaller creatures had used the bridge to cross from one side to the other, so the mud at both ends of the bridge was covered with animal tracks. The temperature was dropping. The top of the bridge was becoming icy.

The mother mammoth could tell that her baby was exhausted from all the running, so she stopped near the south end of the log bridge. The little male stood beside her, panting and knees shaking. The other cows stopped and turned to stand on each side of the mother. If they had to fight the wolves, they would fight here.

* * * * *

Margaret ran along the muddy riverbank holding a short throwing spear in both hands. Podi did the same. Right behind them came Tur and Rom, each carrying a longer spear. Every few strides Margaret would glance back over her shoulder. The three wolves were following at a trot. They could speed up at any moment and catch the humans. But it was a wolf's nature to chase its prey for a while, so that the victim would tire and be easier to kill when the time was right.

Margaret could see the mammoth family huddled in the distance. "Head for the mammoths," she yelled. They put their heads down and ran as fast as they could. Behind them the three wolves picked up speed.

As the runners closed in on the mammoths, the cows began to stomp their feet and make trumpeting noises. They did not want anyone near the baby, wolf or human.

Suddenly Podi screamed and fell forward. She had tripped in a muskrat hole, twisting her ankle. Rom dropped to a knee next to her and pleaded, "Get up, get up!" Before he could say more, the lead wolf barreled into him, knocking both of them head over heels in the cold mud.

It was the yearling. A more experienced wolf would have bitten Rom as it ran by, and then turned to bite again. But this was the first time the yearling had outrun its parents in a chase, and the youngster was unsure about what to do next. The wolf hesitated before lunging at Rom.

That second of hesitation was all Rom needed. He jabbed at the wolf with his spear and buried the point in the wolf's throat. The big animal made a choking sound and fell over.

The parent wolves paid no attention to the yearling or Rom. They streaked by in pursuit of Margaret and Tur. The white faced male was about to bite Tur on the heel when the mammoths charged.

The cows put their heads down and lumbered forward, the baby trying to keep up behind them. Margaret and Tur flopped to the ground as the mammoths ran by. The cows crashed into the galloping wolves.

The she-wolf bounced off the grandmother mammoth's trunk and went tumbling end over end into the river. The current pushed her up against the log bridge, then she disappeared.

The big male dove underneath the cows and slid forward on his belly. He popped up behind the cows and next to the baby. He opened his mouth wide to sink all of his sharp teeth into the baby's neck.

Two short spears buzzed by the wolf's head. He was startled and turned away from the baby mammoth. Margaret and Tur were up and running, arms spread wide and yelling "Hey, hi-yi-yi hey" at the top of their lungs.

The terrified baby did not know what to do. In panic he backed up until his hind feet were up on the log bridge. The ice made him slip backward and he ended up on his knees in the middle of the bridge. His big eyes were wide with fright. He began to lose his balance.

Margaret shouted, "Tur, help me," and climbed up on the bridge after the baby. Tur followed. They kneeled on each side of the baby's head and put their arms around his neck to steady and calm him. The baby grabbed Margaret's pigtail in his little trunk. He was shivering with fright. "Be brave, little one," whispered Margaret, "we won't let anything hurt you." She closed her eyes, exhaled slowly, and opened her eyes.

Now there were four adult mammoths facing the big male wolf! The bull was standing in front of the three cows, breathing hard. The bull raised his massive trunk and trumpeted, "Bah-rooooooo, bah-rooooooo!" He stomped the ground with his right leg. Margaret could feel the log bridge begin to slide.

The wolf crouched between the bull and the bridge. The wolf snapped and growled at the bull, then turned and growled at Margaret and Tur. He'd traveled a long way to feast on baby mammoth and intended to get what he deserved. Beads of dirt and spit rolled down the white side of the wolf's snout as he gathered himself.

He sprang high toward the bridge.

He sprang high toward the bridge.

The wolf was snatched out of midair. A great swinging tusk caught him under the front legs and sent him rocketing up into the sky. The wolf landed in a heap on the other side of the river and did not move.

The bull stared at the dead wolf for a moment, then turned to look at Margaret and Tur. He made a rumble in the back of his throat.

"Margaret, we need to give the baby back right now, before we end up like that wolf." Tur slowly stood up and gently pulled on the baby's ear. Margaret stood and pulled on the other ear. The baby lifted his head and began to stand. He bleated to his mother. The log bridge started to wobble.

Tur and Margaret carefully guided the baby to the edge of the bridge where his mother stood waiting. She stretched her long trunk toward him, and he his short trunk toward her, and when they touched the baby jumped for the ground. The baby pushed hard with his back feet to make his leap, and when he did the end of the bridge popped loose from the bank. All the logs and sticks and mud, along with Margaret and Tur, tumbled with a tremendous splash into the foaming river.

Margaret's deerskin jumper became caught on the biggest log and she was carried along with her head above water. Tur was not so lucky. A floating stick clubbed him on the back of the head and he disappeared under the surface.

"No, Tur, no!" screamed Margaret. She struggled out of her dress and dove under the dark water. She immediately bumped into Tur. Margaret grabbed a handful of his long hair and kicked as hard as she could for the surface. They popped up next to a floating mat of grass, twigs, and mud. Margaret hugged it like a life preserver with one arm while keeping her other arm around Tur. A nasty bump was swelling up on the back of his head. He mumbled, "Oooohhh."

"Tur, wake up, I'm getting tired. Do you hear me?"

"Whaa – what?" Tur's head was beginning to clear. He blinked the water from his eyes and spit.

Margaret pulled Tur's dagger from behind his back and, reaching as far forward as possible, jabbed it into the middle of the floating sticks. "Now use your knife as a handle and pull yourself out of the water!" Tur slowly reached up and grabbed the handle. He took a deep breath and pulled. He ended up on his belly in the middle of what used to be part of the bridge.

Now it was Margaret's turn. She was growing weak because of the cold water, and because she had used most of her remaining strength to save Tur. She tried to kick one leg up and onto the raft but she was just too tired. She thought, *It would be easy to let go and drift away. Maybe I should . . .*

Suddenly Margaret was grabbed by the wrist and the ankle and awkwardly dragged up on the raft. She ended up in a pile on top of Tur. He looked exhausted.

"Margaret," Tur panted, "welcome to Tur Island!" Then he fainted.

CHAPTER 19
RAFT

The river flowed west and south, away from the Big Ice and the grassy plain. The spindly birch trees and tall grass along the banks slowly gave way to bigger trees and bushes, which protected Margaret and Tur from the north wind.

Still, the castaways were cold and miserable. They were barefoot. Tur had kicked off his warm leggings when running from the wolves. His breeches and shirt were damp and caked in mud. Margaret was wearing only her thin cotton pajamas.

They spent the night huddled together in the middle of the little raft. Tur had a headache and threw up twice. Most of the time he kept his eyes shut and did not speak. When he began to shiver, Margaret held him tight. They stayed that way until the rising sun began to warm the air.

After daybreak Tur started to feel better. He sat up, looked around, and began giving orders.

"Before the current takes us much farther, we need to stop and walk back up stream."

"Why?"

"Before the wolves attacked, Rom wanted to head back to the Gathering. He and Podi will wait for us a little while, but that's all."

"Well, let's paddle over to the shore. I need some privacy."

They lay on their stomachs and paddled with their arms. Slowly, in fits and starts, they steered the raft to shore. Tur grabbed some ironwood branches that were sticking out over the water. "Jump," he told Margaret. "I'll follow in a minute." Margaret sprang onto the dry ground and ran behind some bushes. Back on the raft Tur used his dagger to cut walking sticks from the ironwood branches. He intended to lash his dagger to the end of one of the sticks.

Margaret finished her morning business and was looking for something to use as tissue. She noticed a stand of bog cotton tufts waiving in the morning wind. They made a wall of white in front of a very large pine stump. She stood up and walked over to pick some.

As Margaret bent down to pluck a handful of tufts, she heard a snuffling, grunting sound coming from the other side of the pine stump. She crept up to the stump on her hands and knees and peered over the top.

Spread across the marshy earth was the head and neck of a dead elk. Its antlers were at least five feet across! She could see the dead elk's tongue sticking out from corner of its mouth. The body of the elk was nowhere to be seen.

The grunting was coming from a four legged beast that was trying to drag the elk head into a shallow pit. The creature was slightly smaller than a black bear, with a broad round head, little ears, and big shoulders. Except for a mask of silver fur behind its coal black eyes, the animal was covered in thick, dark, oily fur. Each of its paws had five toes and each toe ended in a long claw. At the rear end was a bushy tail. The beast looked up at Margaret and bared a purple mouth filled with sharp white teeth.

Margaret was scared, but not too scared to notice a horrible stink was coming from the brute. It smelled ten times worse than a dead skunk. She slowly turned toward the river, and with a big first leap began to run. The beast lumbered around the pine stump and gave chase.

"T-u-r-r-r," Margaret screamed, "push off, push off!" Taken by surprise, Tur stood with his mouth open, watching Margaret run. When she began to flail her arms above her head, he got the message and pushed the raft away from shore with his new walking stick. Margaret never slowed down but jumped straight out from the river bank and into the water. Tur reached to her with the pole and she grabbed on. He pulled her to safety.

Meanwhile, her stocky pursuer had stopped at the water's edge. It rocked its head back and forth a few times, sniffed the air, and turned back to where it had been interrupted.

Margaret sat on the edge of the raft, trying to catch her breath. Her long hair was soaked so she undid her braids to dry it out. Tur stood at the back of the raft, pushing his pole and grinning.

"What's so funny?" she asked.

"Margaret, where in the world did you find that ke'kaju?"

"Ke-kaw-what?"

"Ke'kaju; you know, a skunk-bear. He's the meanest thing on four legs and hates everybody, except for lady ke'kajus. If you ever come across another, walk away quietly and leave him alone."

"Thanks for the warning. I'm hungry. What should we do about breakfast?"

"Try a couple of these." He bent over and picked something up from a pile at the back of the raft. "I found them in a fresh mound of dirt at the edge of the river. You can poke them open with my knife." He dropped what looked like two leathery ping pong balls into her cupped hands. "They're turtle eggs. You'll like them."

Tur handed Margaret his knife. She poked a hole in the first egg, lifted it to her mouth, and sucked out the insides. It was almost all yolk and very eggy. Margaret sucked down the second egg. A few seconds after the eggs were in her stomach, her mouth filled with a musky aftertaste, almost like mud. But she was so happy to eat something that she didn't mind.

Margaret handed the knife back to Tur and he quickly slurped down three eggs. Some of the yolk ran down his chin. Margaret scooped a floating leaf from the surface of the river to wash him off.

"So what do we do now?" Margaret asked Tur as she wiped his chin.

"Thanks. We've traveled quite a ways, mostly west and south, and I'm not sure of the way back to Da and Ma. People like to fish, so maybe we should float along until we meet somebody. They might help us get home."

For the first time in a while, Margaret felt homesick.

CHAPTER 20
RAPIDS

Margaret and Tur floated down the middle of the widening river on their raft for a night, a day, and another night. The night sky was filled with stars, a great number of them shooting stars. The youngsters lay on their backs, hands folded, and looked up.

"I've never seen so many shooting stars," Tur said in a hushed voice. "Do you think they're happy spirits or angry spirits?"

"I don't think they're spirits at all, just a big cloud of meteors," Margaret replied.

"Not that again! Mee-tee-oar." Tur made a goofy face when he said 'meteor.' "Margaret, *everybody* knows stars are spirits. One of them might be Gam. Maybe that one!" Tur pointed to the east, where dawn was breaking. A bright yellow-white light glowed just above the horizon.

"My da, Joe, says that one's a planet - Venus, I think. He says Venus can help you hold a course when you're lost. Right now it tells me the river is taking us south."

Tur did not argue. Instead, he grabbed his steering pole and stood up. "Something moved in the brush on the left bank."

"Maybe a deer?" Margaret suggested.

"No, I don't think so." Tur squinted and stared. "For a moment I thought I saw –"

A pine cone came flying out of the bushes and zipped past Tur's left ear.

"What . . .?"

A second pine cone followed, hitting Tur square in the chest.

"Ow!"

"Tur, get down!" Margaret grabbed Tur around the waist and pulled him to the deck. He lost his grip on the steering pole and it disappeared into the dark water.

"Look," Margaret pointed toward the shore, "there's the boy who's throwing things at us!"

On the shore was a boy, Tur's age or a year or two older, with an eagle feather in his hair, yelling and pointing downstream. He was so far away that Margaret and Tur could not understand what he was shouting. Up ahead there was a sharp bend in the river, so they could not see what was upsetting the stranger. He began to run at top speed along the bank, going in the same direction as the current, and disappeared into some tall brush.

The current began to speed up, and pushed the raft toward a rocky point that stuck out into the river right before the big bend. Margaret was sitting cross legged in the middle of the raft. Tur had stood up and was holding Margaret's shoulders to steady himself. Margaret could hear a deep rumbling sound coming from beyond the rocky point.

"Tur, what's that sound?" She turned her head to look up at Tur. His eyes were wide open with fright.

"Rapids, it's rapids!" he croaked. "We gotta get off this raft before it breaks up on the big rocks!"

With that, the raft slammed into the end of the rocky point and bounced away like a piece of cork. Now they could see around the bend. Directly ahead, stretching from one bank of the river to the other, was a line of boulders. The rumbling noise became a roar as the water rushed between the big round rocks, splashing up magnificent sprays of white foam. Margaret wanted to scream, but her mouth was so dry she couldn't make a sound.

A short spear flew out of the brush and stuck with a wet thud in the tail of the raft. The spear was tied to a rope that stretched back to the end of the rocky point, where it was looped around a tree stump. The boy with the eagle feather in his hair had braced himself against the stump, trying with all his might to keep the rope from slipping.

Tur leaped at the life line, landed on his belly, and wrapped the wet rope around his forearms before it could unwind from the spear. To keep Tur from being pulled into the water, Margaret grabbed his ankles and sat down hard in the middle of the raft. She spread her legs and wedged her heels between the logs. The weight of the raft and the force of the current stretched the rope tight as a wire. The front of the raft began to scrape against a huge green boulder.

"Pull!" Margaret screamed at the boy on the rocks. "Pull!"

The boy strained backwards with the dry end of the rope wrapped around his waist. With each step the raft got a few feet closer to shore and a few feet farther from the green boulder.

The rope was rubbing Tur's arms raw. "I don't know how much longer I can hold on," he shouted.

"Just a little longer," Margaret shouted back. "We are almost close enough to jump to shore! Get ready to - - "

Margaret did not finish because at that moment a fiery ball no bigger than an apple hurtled down from the sky and crashed into the river next to the big green boulder. Like marbles on the playground, the streaking meteor knocked the big green boulder loose. The boulder began to roll downstream with the current, creating a whirlpool. The nose of the raft ground into the river bottom and the tail of the raft shot straight up. Tur was thrown toward the river bank into water up to his waist. The current was very strong so only his hold on the rope kept him from being swept downstream. Tur reached out toward Margaret and yelled "Take my hand." Still sprawled on the raft, she tried to reach back. But then the raft flipped over, and she disappeared.

CHAPTER 21
RESCUE

When the raft flipped over, Margaret was sucked through the hole left by the rolling boulder. She kept her mouth closed but rushing water filled her nose. The water smelled like burnt toast, then mint, and was filled with thousands of red bubbles. She waited until her toes touched gravel at the river bottom and then she pushed with all her might toward the surface.

Margaret popped to the surface gasping for air, her eyes covered with her long wet hair. She could still hear Tur yelling "Take my hand!" so she blindly thrust her right arm toward his voice.

"Gotcha!" A strong grip found Margaret's hand and pulled her onto the river bank. She landed on her back with a thud.

"Are you all right?"

Margaret sat up, brushed her hair from her face, and replied, "I think so. That was close! Tur, where's the boy who – "

A tall boy was standing over her, but he was not Tur. He asked, "Can you stand?" He reached down to help her up.

Margaret was unsteady on her feet and fell against her rescuer. He had thick dark hair, brown eyes, and was wearing a red tee shirt and khaki cargo shorts. The front of his shirt read *Camp Staff, Gerber Scout Reservation.* And behind his right eye was a small birthmark shaped like a star.

Two younger boys, about Mutt's age, came running up. One was a pale redhead covered with freckles and the other had short black hair and skin the color of dark coffee. Each was wearing a grubby Boy Scout tee shirt and holding a fishing pole. The redhead exclaimed, "Tom, does she need first aid, huh, does she?"

"Well, I don't know, let's ask her," said the tall boy. Grinning, he asked Margaret, "Would you like to help these Scouts earn a first aid merit badge?"

Margaret looked down at the eager youngsters. Neither one had washed his face, neck or fingernails lately. "No, thank you," answered Margaret, "but could you please tell me who you are and where I am? And I've lost a friend. We were on a raft together. My name's Margaret."

"Tom," said the tall boy. They shook hands. Tom told the younger boys, "Run back to the campsite and tell your Scoutmaster that you pulled a lost girl out of the river, and that she has a missing friend." The boys dashed away.

The air was warmer than before Margaret had fallen in the river. She could hear people laughing and smelled hot dogs cooking on a charcoal grill. Two teenage girls in bathing suits went paddling by in kayaks. And immediately downstream a huge mound of dirt, topped by a road, stretched from one side of the wide river to the other.

"Where did that come from?" asked Margaret in surprise.

"Oh, that's Hardy Dam," explained Tom. "It was built across the river during the Depression. My great grandpa says that before the dam was built, there were rapids here, but they got covered when the water backed up behind the dam."

Margaret felt more and more confused. "What day is it?"

"It's the Saturday before Labor Day. I've been working at a Scout camp all summer and brought the boys to Hardy Pond for one last day of fishing before school starts and the camp closes. You scared my Scouts to death when you popped out of the water like an angry beaver. I told them beavers don't get that big."

Oh yes they do, thought Margaret.

The two younger boys returned, out of breath, and the redhead gasped, "Our Scoutmaster called the cops on his cell phone. He said to bring Margaret back to camp."

"Can we make a stretcher to carry you up the hill?" the other boy asked eagerly.

"No, thanks," said Margaret. "I can make it on my own."

* * * * *

Joe Gale burst through the front doors of the hospital's emergency ward and sprinted up to the front desk.

The nurse supervisor on duty looked up from her computer screen and asked, "May I help you?"

"My name's Gale, Joe Gale. I got a call from the County Sheriff that my daughter, Margaret, was found and brought here. Is she OK? Can I see her?" Joe was gripping the edge of the counter so tightly that his knuckles were turning white.

"Yes, Mr. Gale, your daughter is here. I'm told she's fine. The doctor is with her now. If you'll follow me I'll take you to her room."

Joe sighed with relief, wiped tears from his eyes with the back of his hand, and quietly replied, "Thanks." He followed the nurse down the hall to Margaret's room.

The door was partly open and Joe could see Margaret sitting up in bed. She looked freshly bathed and was wearing a crisp blue hospital gown. A young woman doctor was looking into one of Margaret's ears with a small flashlight. *Margaret's so tan,* thought Joe, *and her hair is so long. She doesn't look like a little girl anymore.* Joe took a deep breath and stepped into the room.

"Daddy!" Margaret squealed. Joe rushed to her and gave her a bear hug. "Are you all right, Sweetheart. Are you hurt?" *I thought you were dead!*

"She's in fine health," said the doctor. "Just some minor scrapes from falling in the river. And thick calluses on her feet from going barefoot all summer." The doctor offered her hand. "I presume you're Dad?"

Joe shook the doctor's hand. "Yes. Joe, Joe Gale."

"I'm Doctor Cardea. I need to go next door and check on another patient. You and I will talk again before you take Margaret home. Somebody will be in shortly with new clothes for Margaret. I'm afraid her old things were so ragged they fell apart when we tried to wash them."

That's because I lost the good jumper that Gam made for me, thought Margaret.

After the doctor left, Margaret talked Joe's ear off for a half hour. She told him a fantastic tale of Indians and giant animals and a dangerous journey to something called "the Big Ice." It was almost impossible for Joe to take it all in. He was still getting used to the idea that Margaret was *alive.*

A nurse's assistant showed up with a clean hoodie and some running shorts for Margaret to wear home. Margaret asked the assistant to help braid her hair. *That's odd,* thought Joe, *I don't remember her wearing braids before.* He left the room so Margaret could get dressed.

Dr. Cardea met Joe in the hallway. "I've got Margaret's discharge papers right here and you may leave when she's ready."

"Doctor."

"Yes?"

"My daughter just told me an unbelievable story about how she spent the summer. Is that normal? Will she be alright?"

The doctor stared back at Joe for a few seconds before answering him. "Margaret obviously had a rough summer. She has the sort of deep tan and callouses that we see on homeless people who live outdoors. She was probably scared and alone, with nobody to love her and watch over her. So, her mind invented a story to make it easier for her to get by. I don't think Margaret's suffered any permanent emotional injury to worry about."

Joe's shoulders shook a little as relief washed over him. "Thank you, thank you so very much for finding my girl and taking such good care of her. I suppose her imagination just got the better of her when she was lost."

"You are very welcome," the doctor replied. "Oh, one more thing. I don't know where or how Margaret got the little elephant tattoo on her forearm, but it seems to be healing nicely. To be safe, keep an eye on it for several more weeks. Good bye."

THE END

To My Younger Readers,

The Gathering took place before European people sailed to America, before Jesus walked the hills of Galilee, before the emperors built the Great Wall of China, and before the pharaohs erected the Pyramids.

The mammoth -- and the mastodon, smilodon, giant beaver, dire wolf, giant sloth, American horse and short faced bear -- roamed Michigan for thousands of years. When the Big Ice – today we call it a glacier – started to melt, Indians began to arrive on foot from the west. Then the really big animals disappeared. Some scientists believe the big animals could not stand the warming weather. Others believe the big animals were killed off by Indian hunters. Nobody knows for sure.

A very long time from now, the Big Ice will come back to Michigan. If that happens, let's hope the mammoth will return.

H.G.

To Moms and Dads,

Margaret went back in time to the end of the Pleistocene geological epoch, about 12,000 BP (10,000 BC). The Pleistocene began 2,000,000 BP, and glaciers expanded and contracted across Michigan during that long span of time. In other words, the "Ice Age" had cold spells and warm spells, geologically speaking.

By 12,000 BP, the lower peninsula was mostly free of glacial sheet ice. The west coast of lower Michigan lay several miles west of the eastern shore of modern Lake Michigan. The body of water that would become Lake Huron spread farther inland than the shore of modern Saginaw Bay.

You can use a map of modern Michigan to chart the travels of Margaret and her adopted Paleo-Indian family. Margaret originally appeared to Oogay's family as they fished the Grand River somewhere between Spring Lake (Ottawa County) and Eastmanville (Ottawa County). The family followed the river upstream to Grand Rapids (Kent County), where they saw the dire wolves kill a giant beaver. They were almost to Ionia (Ionia County) when the children watched the smilodons attack and kill the young mastodon.

At Muir (Ionia County) the family branched away from the Grand River and followed the Maple River tributary in a northeast direction. Eventually they picked up the Bad River and followed it into the Shiawassee Flats. The Gathering took place just north of St. Charles (Saginaw County).

The trek to the Big Ice started at the Gathering and ended at what is now Houghton Lake and the headwaters of the Muskegon River (Roscommon County). Margaret and Tur rode their raft down the Muskegon as far as the present day location of Hardy Dam (Newaygo County). Margaret was reunited with Joe at the community hospital in Fremont (Newaygo County).

Margaret's circle of exploration and adventure consumed the entire summer before her sixth grade year. When she returned to school in September, her class was given the usual assignment of writing down what they had accomplished during the summer. At parent-teacher conferences in October, Margaret's teacher told Joe that his daughter had "quite an imagination."

H.G.

ACKNOWLEDGMENTS

I am grateful to the many friends who helped with the creation of this story. They include: Jaime Alvarez, Director of Public Relations, Rosamond Gifford Zoo; Dillon H. Carr, PhD, Assistant Professor of Anthropology, Grand Rapids Community College; Michelle Dixon; Nancy Wagner; Mary Cotterall, Reading Specialist, Spring Lake Public Schools; and Mary VandenBosh's fourth graders at Holmes Elementary School. My wife, Laura, knows better than anyone why I wrote this story now.

ABOUT THE AUTHOR

Henry Granger writes novels about historical events that happened in his home state of Michigan. He and his wife reside where the Grand River flows into Lake Michigan.

Made in the USA
Columbia, SC
30 May 2018